I0724925

Spirit Guide
Madame Chalamet Ghost Mysteries 3

Byrd Nash

ROOK AND CASTLE PRESS
SAINT CHARLES, ILLINOIS

Publisher's Cataloging-in-Publication Data
provided by Five Rainbows Cataloging Services

Names: Nash, Byrd, author.
Title: Spirit guide : a gaslamp ghost mystery / Byrd Nash.
Description: Saint Charles, IL : Rook and Castle Press, 2023. | Series: Madame Chalamet ghost mysteries, bk. 3.
Identifiers: ISBN 978-1-954811-53-9 (Amazon paperback) | ISBN 978-1-954811-54-6 (IngramSpark paperback) | ISBN 978-1-954811-07-2 (Kindle ebook) | ISBN 978-1-954811-13-3 (EPUB)
Subjects: LCSH: Women detectives--Fiction. | Ghosts--Fiction. | Kidnapping--Fiction. | Fantasy fiction. | Detective and mystery stories. | Paranormal romance stories. | BISAC: FICTION / Fantasy / Gaslamp. | FICTION / Fantasy / Romance. | FICTION / Romance / Paranormal / General. | FICTION / Mystery & Detective / General. | GSAFD: Mystery fiction. | Fantasy fiction. | Occult fiction. | Love stories.
Classification: LCC PS3614.A724 S65 2023 (print) | LCC PS3614.A724 (ebook) | DDC 813/.6--dc23.

Contents

Books by Byrd Nash

Madame Chalamet Ghost Mysteries

Ghost Talker #1

Delicious Death #2

Spirit Guide #3

Gray Lady #4

Haunted Grave #5

Ghastly Mistake #6

Contemporary, Magical Realism

A Spell of Rowans

College Fae Series

Never Date a Siren #1

A Study in Spirits #2

Bane of Hounds #3

Romantic Fairytales

Dance of Hearts (Cinderella retelling)

Price of a Rose (Beauty and the Beast retelling)

Fairytale Fantasy

The Wicked Wolves of Windsor and other Fairytales

*"-when you have eliminated the impossible,
whatever remains, however improbable,
must be the truth?"*
The Sign of Four, Sherlock Holmes

Dedications
To the one who loves ghosts.

Chapter One

For someone who said she was never wrong, Twyla Andricksson made mistakes rather often. For example, instead of summoning the spirit of a suicidal servant, she materialized a ghost of a completely different sort.

"Twyla, please send him back. *Immediately.*"

"I'm trying, Madame Chalamet. I'm really trying!" the girl wailed.

"I took her by the throat and throttled her until her eyes burst," said the ghost gleefully. The creature stood behind Jacques Moreau's chair, leering at us all, his eyes gleaming manically.

Mysir Vonn's nefarious doings had been sensational at the time, forcing the city into a panic. After a manhunt, he'd been shot by a guardia when the spree killer was found crouching over the body of one of his victims. Since then, Vonn had reached mythic status as a bogeyman to scare women into not traveling out at night or down dark streets.

Out of patience, I snapped, "Would-you-please-shut-up, Mysir Vonn? No one is interested in hearing about your nasty crimes."

The ghost ignored me. "She displayed her breasts shamefully, wantonly. I was forced to punish her."

The room was dark; the only light was from the candle at the center of the table, which illuminated the face of the mother of the dead servant girl. She was beet red from angry embarrassment. "I want you to know my girl was a sweet innocent! There were no breasts being displayed, mysir!"

"Madame Chapelle, this ghost has nothing to do with your daughter. Give Mys Andricksson a moment, and she will get it all straightened out."

As a child I had wished for a pony, only for those naïve hopes to be dashed. My optimism suffered again now. Apprenticed unasked to me by Parnell Lafayette of the Morpheus Society, Twyla Andricksson continued trying in vain to dismiss our vile interloper.

She was seated on my left, and Madame Chapelle to my right. Since Jacques was in town, he had come along. He held the hands of Twyla and Madame Chapelle, and from across the table he wiggled his eyebrows at me, clearly amused at how things were going.

"Did you try the dismiss sequence, Mys Andricksson?" The mental exercise for disengaging from a malevolent spirit was one of the core pieces we studied in our training. It was basic, but effective. The girl should know it.

"Yes," the girl said, but under my stern eye she wilted. "I mean no. Truth is, I don't remember much about it. So much comes to me naturally that studying wasn't really necessary. I just skipped to the interesting bits. I could try summoning a demon to dispatch him?"

"*No!*"

The horrible entity continued. "I used my knife—"

Not being the medium who had summoned him, there was only one quick way for me to end this. I stood up, dropping my hands to break the circle. When I turned up the gaslamp, the room became bright again, vanquishing shadows. Without the circle of intention to power it, the ghost faded away from the earthly plan, its essence retreating to the Beyond.

"Mys Andricksson, please clean up Madame Chapelle's dining table." To our hostess, I said, "I'm so sorry things didn't work out in talking with your daughter tonight. Sometimes the spirits can be difficult."

"Oh, I imagine so." The housewife eyed Twyla askance as the girl accidentally knocked over the brass candlestick we had used, dropping melted wax on her tablecloth. I suppressed a sigh of tired frustration. *This girl!* "But that other fella? He ain't coming back, is he?"

"No. I'll make sure of that by installing protections before we leave. But if he does, let me know right away and I'll return to take care of him."

"Alright, but what about my girl? I wanted to know she was alright."

"If you can give me something of hers on loan, I will see if I can find her myself when things are quieter."

After her experience with us tonight, I wouldn't have been surprised if she'd said no. But her desperation was great. "She had a locket. Mind you, I'll be wanting it back."

"Of course."

When she left the room to get it, Jacques stood up and stretched before retrieving his hat and cane where they were resting on the couch. "That was entertaining."

Lean and tan, almost sun-burned, his red-gold hair bright as a polished penny, Jacques was in Alenbonné due to military leave. When he had stopped by the Crown hotel this afternoon, I had suggested he come with us, thinking that a bit of male energy might do the séance good. That had been a mistake, for it seemed his presence made my apprentice even more nervous.

"Entertaining, but not enlightening. A mother still doesn't have comfort." The last was said as a chastisement to my apprentice. Parnell Lafayette was probably laughing over the fact that he had saddled me with such a dimwit. I could not refuse the indenture, as it was required by the Society that we mentor other junior members, and I had already gone several years without participating as a guide. I was overdue and would need to endure it.

Jacques did not take Twyla's failure very seriously, which further irritated me. "She'll do better next time in calling the right spook."

"Fine for you to say, but *you* don't have to beg Madame Chapelle for forgiveness."

"Let the girl do that. Old women will forgive youth anything." He kissed my cheek in farewell. "Look, I've got to run."

"Cards or a woman?"

He grinned, his teeth flashing white against his bronze face. "If you must know, dinner at the club with a few of the boys coming in from Zulskaya. They're only here tonight before they take ship in the morning, heading to Perino to replace my lot."

"Before you rush away, would you call me and Mys Andricksson a quick-cab? I don't want to roam up and down the street at night in this neighborhood looking for one."

"Certainly."

Madame Chapelle returned, her hands gripping a long chain that dangled between her chapped fingers. It was a cheap brass locket. "Her dearest possession. From her father."

"Let me write you a receipt for it."

Unlike someone from a higher station, she did not waffle about not needing a receipt or that she trusted me. She was of the working class, a laundry woman I imagined, who always asked for proof that bills had been paid.

From my bag, I took pencil and paper and wrote hastily on it, giving a brief description, my signature and the date. "Here, madame. Now if you will let me, I shall put some protections at your doors and windows."

Jacques gave her a bow, his tricorn hat tucked under his arm. "Duty calls, madame, but thank you for letting me enjoy your delightful home for the evening." Madame Chapelle showed him to the door, which was in the hall right outside her parlor.

It took a little longer for Twyla to finish cleaning up the candle wax and brazier used to burn the herbs well-suited to a séance. As she repacked my bag, I went with Madame Chapelle around her small home, the bottom flat of a three-storey building, and set protections at her door and windows to put her mind at ease.

After all of it was done, and more reassurances given, we bade our client goodbye. Gripping Twyla under her elbow, I propelled her out the door and into a waiting carriage at the curb of Madame Chapelle's boarding house.

"Do I have homework for you, Mys Never-Studied-A-Day-In-Your-Life!" I snapped. I was so blinded by my anger at Twyla's unprofessionalism that it took a moment to realize that we had entered a coach, not a cab, and that it was already occupied.

From the recesses of the carriage, Mysir de Archambeau said, "I see Anne-Marie was correct about where we might find you."

I gave a start of surprise, for I had not seen the Duke de Archambeau since the Winter Revels. That surprise was followed by irritation; the man had a habit of disappearing and popping up like a rabbit in a conjuring act. It seemed we had entered the duke's own coach, but the one without his coat of arms, and thus anonymous. Next to him sat a man I did not know.

"Your Grace, whatever are you doing here?" I asked, settling in the seat next to Twyla, opposite the two men.

He rapped the hilt of his cane on the roof, and the carriage started off. "Baron Losendahl, meet Madame Elinor Chalamet, Ghost Talker. The girl with the mouth hanging open is her apprentice, Mys Twyla Andricksson."

"Pleased to make your acquaintance," said the blond giant gruffly.

With his eyes gleaming, the duke said, "Why don't you tell us why we are here? Why we have sought you out, Madame Chalamet?"

Analytically, I examined Baron Losendahl. From his appearance, I discerned several things. He was a newcomer to the city and was a native to Zulskaya, that mountainous, snowy country to the northeast of my own Sarnesse. The baron was as broad as a barn, his shoulders a thick beam, his head and neck making one solid bullet shape. His nose had been broken once in the past, and he wore thick mutton chops.

"Did you leave your mountains to come to consult me? No. That alone would not entice a man of your station and wealth. You would have sent for me to come to you. That's what the rich do. It is another who brings you here to our fair city. A wife? No, daughter— yes, a daughter who is in trouble in Alenbonné, and you requested your old friend, the Duke de Archambeau, to recommend someone to help you in this sensitive matter."

"Madame! How do you know this?" said the baron in astonishment.

The duke leaned back, smiling, as I explained.

"Your accent tells me you are from Zulskaya, though your cravat pin has the emblem of a well-known Alenbonné sporting club for le beau idéal who enjoy boxing and fencing. I have seen such an insignia at the duke's private residence, a cup engraved with a win of over twelve years ago. Hence the long friendship. Also indicative that you are not the type of man who would entrust your secrets to just any casual acquaintance.

"It is a sport you continue to enjoy, for the skin of your knuckles is reddened from bare-knuckle fighting, probably as recently as last night. But your face remains unbruised, so it was a match and not a street fight. Probably an exercise to work out some great frustration."

The baron looked at Archambeau, who only remained silent in his corner. He turned back to me and confided, "You are correct, madame. But what about my recent arrival? How did you come by that?"

"You took off your hat during our introductions. That showed not only manners but also the inside of the band, which has the name of the maker— a decent shop for men's general attire located in Needle District, but not the best. It specializes in the ready-made, so this was bought when you arrived here. It is too small for your head, as I can tell by the mark across your forehead. A head your size would need a custom-made chapeau."

Archambeau's smile had become a smirk as I continued.

"Meanwhile, your tailored and expensive coat is made of kalukoo wool, which is native to the mountains of Zulskaya. It is not often seen in Sarnesse because of the high import tax, yet the garment fits your shoulders like a glove. The wear marks at the cuff and lapels show you have owned it for at least two seasons."

"No! I do not believe this. Someone has told you about my daughter and her plight. How else would you know?"

"If it were a matter of government, the duke would not need me. If it was a public matter, you would consult Inspector Marcellus Barbier, who is a very fine guardia detective known to the duke. No, His Grace brings you here instead of waiting for me to return to the Crown, as it is an urgent matter or one that requires discretion. Hence a family matter."

"That's cracking!" cried my protégé, clasping her hands together in excitement. "Why don't you teach me how to do *that*?"

"Because it requires you to use logic and deductive reasoning, Twyla. Something you seem to lack!"

The baron tried to find a flaw in my logic. "My quest could have been for a son, not a daughter."

"It could have been. But a son you would wait to return, tail between his legs, begging for forgiveness after a debauchery. A daughter? She requires immediate rescue."

"I told you she was good," murmured the duke from his corner, giving me a little clap of appreciation with hands in dove-gray gloves. "Now, will you take the case?"

"Of course."

"Even if it is against your own kind?" growled the baron.

"I help all. Without prejudice," I replied calmly to his outburst.

Glancing sideways at my apprentice, the duke expounded upon the baron's remark. "It involves the Morpheus Society."

"Well, of course I'm still a member in good standing, but I have served my years as a journeyman and my time is now my own."

"But what of your loyalty?" demanded the baron.

"My loyalty is to my client, as long as you are not asking me to do anything illegal or unethical. Now, Mys Andricksson is an apprentice, and she is still bound closely to the Society's rules. Let us not speak of this further until we return her to her accommodations."

"Madame!" cried Twyla. "But I want to know."

"And children want to know what they will get for their birthday present, my girl. That doesn't mean their parents relent." I had already been embarrassed by Twyla in front of a washerwoman; I didn't wish to repeat another gaffe in front of nobility, and certainly not in front of Archambeau who would probably never let me live it down.

"Where do we take the girl?"

After I'd told the duke her address, he called up to his driver, and as we changed direction, my apprentice crossed her arms, fuming.

Ignoring her, I asked Archambeau, "How is your mother, and Lady Fontaine? Doing well, I hope."

The duke gave his small smile. "Valentina and Mother are off to the south beaches. It's watercolor season."

"By chance, did Lady Baudelaire go with them?"

At the mention of the woman who had commanded a Ghost Hunt in his house at the first dinner party I had attended there, the duke's eyes grew sardonic.

"She did. She and her husband like to play the casinos, which open on the first day of spring. So my house is my own for a few weeks. We saw Jacques Moreau hail you a cab, but told the driver we would give you a ride instead."

"Yes, I invited him to the séance. Did Anne-Marie not tell you?"

"No, she did not. Only the address and that you were working."

The carriage stopped and, without further ado, I bade Twyla goodnight. "When I see you tomorrow, I want you to be able to do the dismiss sequence for a spirit backward and forward. And no reading up on demons, young lady."

With the dark glance that all mothers of teenagers know so well, the girl left the carriage, the hard corner of her valise hitting my knee. It was probably on purpose, but with Twyla's awkwardness it could have been simply an accident. Hard to tell.

As the coach rolled away, putting distance between us and my pouting protégé, I bent forward and, rubbing my hands with excitement, asked, "Now what trouble has your daughter got herself into, Baron Losendahl?"

CHAPTER TWO

From his pocket, Baron Losendahl handed me a daguerreotype in an oval frame. "My Ebbe."

Because of the dimness in the carriage, I brought it close to my eyes to examine it. The girl was older than I had expected— about my own age, with an unsmiling face and serious eyes. Not a girl who would run away on a whim. Ebbe had a wide mouth, high cheekbones, and hair that curled, by nature or design. From the height of the chair in the daguerreotype, the woman looked to be tall; she had broad shoulders and square hips.

"Is this recent?"

"Taken last year," said her father as I returned it to him. "Let me explain—"

And so Baron Losendahl began his story.

"Ebbe is my oldest child, one of four. Her other three siblings are all brothers and she grew up in a rough and tumble way, hunting and shooting alongside them. She even learned to fence, though I drew the line at boxing— a sport I enjoy, as you noticed.

"My wife and her sister said the girl needed female companionship of her own age. They demanded I send her away to a school where she could be polished, readying her for a good marriage.

"Reluctantly, I agreed. She left for a ladies' seminary with a good reputation when she was about fourteen. While there, she became friends with a young woman named Labrenda Elstad. They became extremely close, and Mys Labrenda visited our home in Zulskaya several times during the summer school breaks.

Here his voice became mildly disdainful. "She was a sweet girl, delicate. Certainly not up for the rough country sports our family enjoyed. A book reader who spent her time pressing flowers.

"During Ebbe's last year at the seminary, however, tragedy struck. Mys Labrenda died in a hunting accident, breaking her neck when her horse took a jump wrong. Our Ebbe was devastated. Inconsolable. She felt herself to be at fault, for she had encouraged the girl to be more bold and daring in her actions, and I'm told picked the horse for the girl to ride that day.

"Although this happened over ten years ago, I mention it because the death of her school friend may have played a part in what has happened recently. Afterward, it fostered a moroseness in her that continues to this day. She gained a morbid curiosity about death, and her fascination was so marked that I forbade her the hunt.

"She finally stopped wearing mourning a few years ago, and last year we hoped she would accept an offer from a young Sarnesse man, Mysir Karl Solberg. He was visiting the area, staying with mutual friends, and the two seemed to come to some understanding.

"Ebbe arranged with a few girlfriends from her academy days to visit Alenbonné, to do some shopping. She insisted on traveling here alone and, since my wife was recovering from a recent illness, we allowed it. After she left, we received this letter."

From his pocket, he brought forth a folded document and

handed it to me. I held it up to the window, using the passing street lamps to read it.

Dear Mother and Father:

What I am about to write may surprise you, but please be assured, my dearest ones, that it fulfills my deepest wishes and desires. When Karl told me about a group of intellectuals in Alenbonné that studied life after death, it was as if the darkness that weighed me down since Labrenda's tragic accident finally lifted. I could finally see my path.

Do not despair for me. Rather, understand that I have found my true calling in joining their illustrious order. The Morpheus Society promises freedom at last from all of my sad troubles.

Your loving Ebbe

"You have contacted the would-be lover— this Karl Solberg?" I asked, refolding the letter and handing it back to the baron.

It was the duke who replied. "Yes. We have already seen him. He states they were never engaged and that he has no idea why she would have told her parents such a tale."

"And yet, it was through him that she heard of the Society. Do we believe him to be innocent of any ulterior motive?" I mused.

"He states it was a casual conversation, and he never thought she took it so seriously at the time."

The baron was letting the duke speak, but his hands were gripped tightly into fists resting on his knee.

I asked them both, "Do you believe him?"

"I want to kill the boy!" roared the baron, leaping to his feet and sending the carriage rocking even more than the natural movement the horses caused.

Archambeau said, "All in good time, Viktor. Now sit down before you tip us over into the gutter."

Losendahl did as bidden, but he clearly wasn't happy about it.

I suggested cautiously, "It could have been an innocent remark that struck home, and he did not know of her intentions. Has he seen your daughter since her arrival in Alenbonné?"

"He says not," growled the worried father.

"Did she see these school friends she mentioned?"

"That we did confirm," said the duke. "It seems the two girls met her at the station and brought her to the Royal Hotel, where they had booked her a room. A room she left about three days later, and vanished. She left behind her maid, who disappeared later the next day."

"So there are two missing women? Are you sure we shouldn't be discussing this with Inspector Barbier?"

"Not yet," said the duke. "We need some indication that they did not leave of their own volition. But we both fear we are running out of time."

"Surely you have contacted the Society?"

"Yes, but without satisfaction." Archambeau's face said, *We will speak of this later.*

"Well, it's getting about dinnertime and—"

"You haven't eaten dinner?" demanded Archambeau. "Dinner at the Royal seems called for."

"I'm always up to tasting what the competition can do," I replied.

Once again, orders were given to the coachman.

Perhaps I should not have been finding myself slightly irked that we were three instead of two. It had been months since I had seen Archambeau, and while the case was intriguing and I was happy to help, the baron's company forestalled any personal questions— such as, where had Archambeau been? Why had he not called? Worse, his manner seemed casual, which was confusing considering our last interaction.

Archambeau asked me, "Is Perdersen still seeing Chef Faucher?"

"Gerhard told me it was a passion too hot to survive."

The baron broke into our conversation. "What is this talk all about? Eating? When my dear girl has been taken, gulled by some smarmy supernatural ghost hunters?"

Archambeau was quick to soothe him. "Viktor, Madame Chalamet does her best work on a full stomach. Besides, I am tired of being in this coach, and the most acceptable place to talk with a lady is over an excellent dinner in a respectable restaurant."

He still seemed unconvinced, so I added, "I understand that you both have talked with Mysir Karl and these two ladies, but the hotel staff at the Royal will know more about her stay than any of these three persons and probably be far more honest with us."

Like the Crown, the Royal had a large and well-appointed dining hall. It had the crystal chandeliers, white linens, and attentive servants dressed in black and white. However, the interior was painted a pale yellow, not blue like the Crown, and the cornices were white plaster and not stained oak. There were few windows, as it was a space cut out between Reception and the hallway to the rooms.

The place was busy; it seemed a theater had just ended a popular play, releasing a hungry audience upon the Royal, but finding a seat was not an issue. Rich men with titles could always be accommodated.

Seated, and with food orders placed, we could now concentrate on other matters.

"Fill me in on what happened after you received the letter. What have you done?"

"I immediately sent a telegram to the Royal Hotel, another to Mysir Karl Solberg demanding he answer for his behavior, and two others to Ebbe's friends: Elyna Hummel and Lisette Paquet. Lastly, I sent one to my dear friend here, Tristan Fontaine, and he told me he would contact the gendarmes about the situation."

"To report her missing?"

"Exactly."

"And their response?" This question I put to the duke, who only shrugged.

"The gendarmes do not prevent crimes or even open investigations on what cannot be verified. Ebbe Losendahl is thirty-one years old and well past being a minor. If she decides of her own free will to leave a hotel, they will only start an investigation when they find her strangled and dumped in a canal." At the baron's shocked gasp, he added contritely, "Sorry there, Viktor, of course I didn't mean that would be Ebbe's fate, only that committed crimes are the focus of the gendarmes."

Our drinks and starter arrived, and the conversation paused. The one benefit to being in a traveling carriage was that a discussion could be private. The server left, and the duke reached to take bread out of the basket and started spreading soft cheese across its surface.

"You mentioned that you had spoken to the Morpheus Society. Did you ask if they had heard of her?"

"I spoke with a man who seems to be in charge, a Mysir Parnell Lafayette, who denied ever hearing of her."

In charge? Let us hope not!

"Let me guess: that conversation ended in verbal violence?"

"Let us say a draw. We both decided a retreat to corners was best in order to maintain our dignity." The duke put the cheese toast on my plate and started making a second one for himself.

The baron promised us in a harsh voice, "I can make him talk. Give me a horse and I'll drag the scoundrel."

Goodness, Zulskaya nobles do have a bit of the rough and ready about them.

"I don't believe that will be necessary. I shall talk with the Society myself and see if your daughter has contacted them. But first, I want to speak with this fake suitor and her friends. You say your daughter's maid is also gone. Did she take any of Ebbe's clothes or jewelry with her?"

"We are not sure. While nothing seems to be missing, as far as the baron can tell, who knows what the girl brought with her," the duke told me.

The next course arrived. The chilled spring pea soup tasted heavenly. "Did the maid know anyone in Alenbonné? Or would she return to her family in your part of the country, Baron?"

"She does have family back home, but my wife telegraphed me and said they have not heard from her either. She has no connections in this city. It is not the type of place where a girl from a remote village in Zulskaya would know anyone."

"Is she prettier than your daughter?"

"What has that got to do with anything?" snapped the baron. But at my cocked head and inquisitive stare, he admitted reluctantly, "Yes, she is very pretty."

"When you can catch our waiter's attention, mysir de duke, would you call him over? And have your wallet ready?"

A man of Archambeau's bearing only had to raise an eyebrow for excellent service.

"May I be of assistance?" asked the slender man, bowing slightly forward as if to indicate an intimacy between us in the busy dining hall. He was pleasantly handsome in a non-threatening way, a quality found in all the best male servants.

Archambeau said, "The lady has a question. If you can answer it, I have a tenner for you."

"I will try, mysir." He was all ears.

"Of the female hotel staff, who would you believe is the most envious of others?"

He seemed surprised at my question, probably having expected something food-related. It took him a moment before he replied diplomatically, "It would reflect poorly upon our hotel if we had anyone like that here."

The duke added a second tenner on top of the first. "Strictly confidential, mysir. Understand it won't go past this table. As far as we are concerned, this conversation never happened."

The server slipped the two bills discreetly into this pocket and found his tongue again. "That would be Madame Travers, madame. She was recently demoted from the front desk under the new manager because of jealous gossip."

"So she still works here?"

"Yes, but as the upper floor manager now. She no longer interacts directly with guests but oversees the work by the chambermaids cleaning the rooms."

After he left, I informed the two men, "We will want to speak to her. Can you arrange that? As well as a private room here, where I can question her and the others?"

"We've already questioned them!" said the baron, clearly wanting immediate answers.

His bear paw was on the table, and I reached over and covered it with my own to comfort him. "I know this is worrisome, but often a woman will reveal to another of her kind what she will not tell a man. For now, I promise you that your daughter is not dead."

"How would you know?" he asked testily, evidently a man more comfortable with anger than grief.

"Because when I held her photograph and letter, they gave off the vibration of a living woman. She still lives, Baron Losendahl, but I agree we must move quickly."

What I did not reveal to him was that Ebbe's vibration was dull and listless. Wherever she was, it was not a healthy place.

CHAPTER THREE

The next morning, in my suite at the Crown, my protégé pleaded her case to help in the search for the baron's missing daughter.

"Sorry, but no. It would be best for you to stay out of this until we know how the Society is involved."

If the few months of having Twyla as an apprentice had shown me anything, it was the amazing quickness with which she could talk. She knelt at my feet, her hand on my knee, looking up at me devotedly. I wasn't fooled for a moment!

"Madame Granger told me the tragic story of how you came to the Society in order to avenge your father's murder. It was so touching! Then how you solve crimes with Inspector Barbier. Amazing. I jumped at the chance of training with you. Who would not? It's every girl's dream to talk with those who met horrific endings so you can solve their murder! Mostly my ghosts have died natural deaths."

Her green eyes sparkled as she clasped her hands together in child-like excitement. "Imagine if Ghost Talking could become part of the new science the gendarmes are developing— as essential as fingerprints, bloodstains, or boot impressions! We could be working on the very forefront of developing new techniques."

My raised hand did not stop her speech, and I imagined she had been rehearsing it since we dropped her off at the hostel for professional young ladies last night.

She clasped her hands together, imploring me to relent. "And I would be very useful to have around. I can watch them while you question suspects and give you my impressions of whether or not they are telling the truth. How can I improve my criminal knowledge if you don't take me with you? As your apprentice, I'm here to learn everything, and you're always telling me that I have a lot to learn."

Behind Twyla, the contortions that passed over Anne-Marie's face during this speech would have been funny, except that the girls' animosity had been hard to deal with these last few months. Anne-Marie was two years younger than my apprentice in age, but in experience she was already her senior. I had not realized how much Anne-Marie viewed me as her special property until Twyla had entered our lives, and it was only by continuously promising her that Twyla's presence was only to be endured for a year that Anne-Marie tolerated the girl's presence at all. This did not stop her from making theatrical gestures and expressions behind Twyla's back when warranted by her outrageous behavior.

Only by speaking loudly was I able to stop Twyla's outburst. "Thank you for your offer, but this is a personal matter that I am looking into and not one for the gendarmes."

The girl took a deep breath, filling her lungs in preparation for launching another explanation or plea, so I rushed forward. "What you can do for me is to inventory my herb closet and make a list of what I have, how much, and what I need to resupply."

"That's busy work!" she wailed.

"Important, though. Very important."

Before she could argue further, I quickly put on my hat and stabbed it with a hatpin before grabbing my leather case. I did not know what the day held for us, so it was best to be prepared. Walking very fast down the corridor to the stairs, I went down to the lobby and out of the building.

It was early spring, and some of the trees on the boulevard were beginning to open their pink buds and show fresh green leaves. The morning weather was partly cloudy and a bit brisk in temperature, but it was nothing that a warm jacket and a scarf couldn't protect against.

Not many were out yet, for it was early morning. Delivery trucks were unloading, and I heard the men's cheerful hallos to each other as crates were passed along to shop owners. A flat-topped roof of a narrowboat drifted by on the canal, its chimney stack puffing, as it brought country produce into town.

The Royal was in the same district as the Crown, so it only took ten minutes to walk the few blocks between them. As arranged the night before, I found Archambeau waiting for me in the lobby. He was as impeccably attired as always in a dark blue suit with a gray pin-stripe, his tie a deep burgundy with black spots. His chin was freshly shaved, showing off the hard, lean jaw, and the waves of his dark hair were brushed into place. He was shiny as a new pin.

He was all business, which I had to admit I found disappointing.

"Prompt as usual, Madame Chalamet. We have Mys Losendahl's two childhood friends here, Elyna Hummel and Lisette Paquet. Madame Travers won't be available for an hour because of her shift."

"Baron Losendahl?"

"Not here, as you requested, but he's champing at the bit. I've got my secretary sitting on him, but as you can imagine, Stephan won't be able to hold him long."

Side by side, we went up the grand staircase of the Royal. The carpet runner was a mix of colors in brown and ox-blood red in an alternating diamond pattern and the banister rail was deep, dark walnut, its surface as smooth as satin. Brass pots in a sedate row across the mezzanine held palm plants taller than the duke.

On the second floor, outside a specific door, he paused. "Do you want me in on this?"

"Not now. But could you send up tea and breakfast? With a lot of choices? I don't want them leaving too quickly."

He nodded and left. Taking a deep breath, I entered the Royal's hotel room to meet Elyna and Lisette.

The suite of rooms Archambeau had selected was quite pleasant and airy, with a delicate spring-green and gold striped wallpaper on the walls, and white-painted wood furniture upholstered in dark green velvet. On the fireplace mantel and the sideboard were sprays of early pink tulips. All the brasses shone and in the grate there was a little fire, just enough to cut the slight chill.

I set my case down by a chair and introduced myself. "I'm Madame Elinor Chalamet. I do appreciate you two coming so promptly."

"I'm not quite sure why we are here," said the woman who had introduced herself as Madame Lisette. She was a willowy blond whose bored expression showed little concern for her missing friend. "There's nothing more to say."

"We've told Ebbe's father all that we know," agreed Madame Elyna, a plump partridge of a woman whose hands in her lap nervously played with the fingers of her gloves.

"This won't take long, and I am sure you would want to help me locate Ebbe Losendahl."

"Of course," murmured Lisette in a languid, lazy drawl.

"Oh, yes!" said Elyna, nodding rapidly.

There was a polite knock at the door before it opened. A waiter rolled in a cart complete with teapot, cups, and saucers, along with a display of hothouse strawberries and grapes, muffins, scones, rolls, and bread, with butter and jam.

Food always made a gathering more friendly, especially as it gave everyone something to do with their hands. I poured tea while Elyna filled our plates.

"I've never met Mys Losendahl and was wondering how you would describe her?"

"Ebbe? Not an intellectual, but solid enough. Preferred games over books. Or did when I knew her," said the bored Lisette, who had decided on tea with lemon, but no sugar. "Bossy. Arrogant. Very confident she knew what was right. When things didn't go her way, she'd crack. Like our last year—"

"You can't blame Ebbe for that! Everyone was quite sorry about it all afterward," said Elyna, who had taken so much milk and cream in her tea it was almost white.

I asked softly, "You are speaking of the riding accident? The death of Labrenda Elstad?"

"Over a decade ago now," said Lisette, who had rather melted into her chair. She crossed one long leg over the other in an unlady-like sprawl, giving a slight rhythmic kicking motion with her right ankle under her skirt. I wondered which was the truth— the boredom or the impatience?

Elyna was the talkative one, though she glanced at her companion before speaking. "The accident changed Ebbe. She was always friendly and game for anything, but afterward, she would fly into a rage when someone left their shoes in the hall, or if you made noise while eating your meal."

"Maybe you shouldn't have dumped your things willy-nilly? I tripped over your skis more than once. That would drive anyone to madness. Don't blame Labrenda's death for Ebbe's testiness over that!"

The gazes of the two ladies locked as if challenging each other. Before either could get mired in a dispute unrelated to my topic of interest, I said, "I would like to know more of Ebbe's nature. Is she an impatient one? Quick to make decisions? Or does she think and plan?"

Elyna, for once, took a moment to think over what I'd asked, while Lisette was more decisive. "I wouldn't call her slow, but more of a calculated risk-taker. She never took a fence she didn't think her horse could manage, unlike someone too foolish to figure out the simplest things."

It seemed everything kept circling back to Labrenda's death.

The two women quickly became lost in reminisces about their boarding school, a camaraderie I never experienced since I was sent only to a day school by Father.

"Do you remember, Lisette, when Ebbe stole Madame's wiglet? Right after you told her she could never do it?"

For the first time since I'd entered, Lisette gave a genuine smile. "And hid it up the chimney when the faculty came in to demand which one of us had been the wicked fringe-napper?"

They both enjoyed a bit of a chuckle. I poured a second round of tea and nibbled a biscuit as the two reminisced.

"I'd almost forgotten that." Lisette leaned over to her friend and added, "Remember when Ebbe showed us how to escape from detention using the drainpipe and the apple tree?"

"Or that whipping she took, when she said it wasn't Labrenda who had copied from her, but that she had from Labrenda?"

"She'd do anything for that girl."

Both sighed at the same time. I asked with delicacy, "I know that Mys Elstad died in a hunting accident, but not much more than that. Why would Lady Losendahl blame herself?"

The two women looked at each other. It was Lisette who explained. "It was the horse. Ebbe picked it out, and when Labrenda worried that the beast was too much for her to handle, Ebbe called her a coward before galloping off on her own mount. We tried to tell her that it was simply an accident and that Labrenda was the one who decided to put her foot in that stirrup, but she felt guilty about it."

Both girls sighed over their teacups, looking into them as if they had answers.

"Didn't see her much after we graduated. Only got the required weekly letter, you know."

"As we were taught to do," explained Elyna. "A weekly letter. Too many and you might appear imposing upon an acquaintance. Too little and you could be accused of not doing your duty to your school sisters."

"Could you tell me how Ebbe arranged this trip to Alenbonné?"

"Now, that was a surprise," said Lisette.

Her friend said, "Out of the blue, she wrote me a letter wondering if we could find her a place to stay in the city while she did some shopping."

"So she told you of the wedding?"

"Didn't believe it at first," said Lisette, shaking her head.

Elyna nodded. "Neither of us believed she would marry after losing Labrenda. They were close in that way."

"I see," I said. "But her parents didn't know that?"

"No."

"So you thought the shopping expedition was a ruse?"

"Of some type," said Lisette. "Probably an excuse to escape that dreary backwater where her family lives."

"Her family is very proud of their estate," said Elyna, as if apologizing for her friend's remarks.

"That didn't stop two of her brothers from leaving it," Lisette snapped. "One off to be a spice-buyer traveling the seas, and the other is now a lawyer in the capital of Zulskaya. That Ebbe had to stay behind, looking after her parents when her brothers felt no need to do so, is shameful in my opinion. Why shouldn't she have been allowed to spread her wings a bit?"

"But they were men," Elyna explained patiently. This only made Lisette sneer as she set her teacup aside.

Wanting to forgo an argument, I interjected, "Once she arrived, did she give you any clues on what she was doing here?"

"None," said Lisette firmly.

"No, unfortunately," said Elyna. "She did seem very happy though."

"Happy? I thought secretive," scoffed Lisette. "Spouting all that nonsense about how we all should fulfill our destinies, have a passion that transcends all things. Meanwhile, Elyna has a husband and child. But did Ebbe ask after them? No."

Elyna was quick to compliment her friend. "And Lisette is a writer. She wrote a book about birds that sold very well."

"You don't mean *The Life of the Songbird*, by chance?"

"Yes. Have you read it?" asked Elyna. "It was a bestseller."

"It's been highly recommended to me," I said, thinking of the Marson family and my adventures at Lindengaard during the Winter Revels.

Without a blush and only a bit of a smirk, Lisette chided her friend, "That means she has not read it. Not to worry, Madame Chalamet, I have thick skin."

"Did you get a feeling from her about anything else? Any hints as to her plans?"

Lisette gave her friend a raised eyebrow, which made Elyna blush. "Give it to her. I told you at the time you shouldn't have accepted it."

Ordered by Lisette, Elyna pulled a necklace of Perino pearls from her drawstring purse. Reaching over, I took it in my hands and instinctively examined the pearls' texture and color. They were real, and quite an expensive trifle to give to a friend with whom you only exchanged mandatory letters once a week— and hadn't seen in over ten years.

"Ebbe gave it to me. I didn't ask her for them. She gave them to me," Elyna insisted.

"What Elyna is trying to say, but not very well, is that she didn't steal them. Ebbe did give them to her in my presence, and tried to give me the matching earrings, but I refused them. They were obviously family heirlooms, and I am sure her family will want them back. Especially now, in case they—"

"They find her dead, you mean?"

Both women nodded solemnly.

CHAPTER FOUR

As the two women left down the hotel corridor, Archambeau approached with another woman, whom I assumed from her attire to be Madame Travers. While Elyna and Lisette paid her no attention, Travers noticed them. Her calculating eyes took in their clothes, their hairstyles, and judged them. Yes, this was the type of person I wanted: someone bitter about what she couldn't have.

"Please do come in." Up close, I could see her measuring me, her eyes weighing my appearance and status. I came up short, if her slight sneer was any indication.

She took the seat that Lisette Paquet had vacated, but her pose was one of stiff discipline, not of practiced ennui.

Madame Travers wore the traditional black of a servant, though the material was of a more expensive kind than usually seen, with embellishments of ruching down the sleeve and lace at the collar. Her figure was contained and forced into the older corset style of the hourglass.

Around her neck was a simple gold chain attached to a round locket pinned high, right under her right collarbone. Probably a timepiece. At her corseted waist was a belt, her chatelaine, and from it her hotel keys dangled.

Madame Travers' features were striking; her green eyes were framed in black eyelashes so thick they marked the area around the eye like a crayon. Her thick hair was swept back from a heart-shaped face that was a little spoiled by the deep, melancholy brackets that went from the edge of her nostrils to the corners of her mouth. Her pale cheeks were artificially tinted, and the redness of her lips had been enhanced. A rather imperial beauty, I imagined.

I invited the duke to remain, offering both some tea.

"No thank you," Madame Travers said stiffly. "I would prefer to get this interrogation over with as soon as possible so I can return to my work."

"Interrogation? I have no plans to conduct one."

Her grievance was plain to see in how the lines on her face deepened. "Why am I here if it is not to chastise me? Or to complain? My employer demanded that I hold myself ready to answer any of the duke's questions."

I put the tea tray back in order from my last visit, returning the lid to the sugar bowl. "I am sorry, but you are mistaken. We are not here to cast blame. We only want to know more about a guest who stayed here at the Royal recently. Your information would be of supreme interest and help a worried father."

"I presume you are speaking of Lady Losendahl."

"Yes." Of course she would have guessed my purpose here, seeing Elyna and Lisette leaving my room. Probably the mysterious disappearance of Ebbe was a nine-days' wonder in the servant's quarters.

"What do you want to know?" Madame Travers' beauty could not gild her harsh voice with the coarse vowels of someone who had been raised without the benefit of a schoolroom education. Her manner was also not pleasing or subservient, such as you would expect in the hospitality trade. No wonder she had been removed from the front desk.

"I can tell you nothing, as I had little to do with the lady. Managing this floor keeps me quite busy; I oversee the work of three chambermaids."

"We are told you are the most observant and intelligent of all the staff here," said the duke, lying shamelessly. He was seated in Elyna's chair, legs crossed and hands resting calmly in his lap. For anyone coming into the room, he was a gentleman of le beau idéal, a man who had a life of leisure, without a care in the world. "It would be a shame if we can't reward you like we did the others."

Unsurprisingly, the promise of financial compensation made Madame Travers re-think her position. The calculation I had seen in her eyes earlier returned. The tip of her tongue licked her lips, as if she were a kitchen kitty discovering the morning delivery of cream.

"Well, I might know one or two things."

The duke gestured, encouraging her to continue. "Anything you can tell us will remain confidential, Madame Travers."

It turned out that for someone who knew nothing, Madame Travers had plenty to share.

"Lady Losendahl arrived late last Monday, with very little baggage considering she had booked the room for a week. I noticed that immediately. Usually that means someone is sending trunks by another train, still to arrive, but nothing ever did. No matter what anyone says, I don't think she had plans to stay long."

"That is very informative," said Archambeau, and she smiled under his encouragement. For now, I would let him lead the conversation; Travers obviously responded best to a man's interest.

She refused the cup I had handed her, but when the duke passed it to her, she accepted it with a smile. Yes, she was a woman who would only bend to a man; for women she had little use.

She took a sip and, after returning it to its saucer, said, "It was obvious she was waiting for someone. Always asking if there were messages for her at the front desk and looking over the stairwell, down to the lobby. When her friends arrived— the two women who passed us in the hall— I thought it was them, but after their lunch she was back to looking over the stair banister and glancing out the windows."

"Did the person ever arrive, do you think?" asked the duke, curiously.

"No. In my opinion, that's why she left. To meet a man who'd not come to her, to this public place where he would be seen. Probably a man her family would disapprove of, and someone she didn't want her nice lady friends to see. A rogue, some ne'er-do-well. These le beau idéal women are always the same with their lovers, thinking we don't know what they're up to."

Archambeau stiffened at her words, his face hardening, for she had unwittingly touched upon his own affairs. Feeling a suspicion growing in me, I asked nonchalantly, "Perhaps you can tell us something about her maid, Mys Hannah Wahl?"

The sneer in her voice became more pronounced. "Like her lady, waiting for her lover, but at least *he* came. Mysir Karl."

"Mysir Karl Solberg is courting Lady Losendahl."

She gave a laugh like a rock dragged on a rope across cobblestones. "You high folk always think you know, but it's us, the servants, who see everything. Mysir Karl might act like he's a gentleman, but he is not past forcing a kiss on a woman on the servant's stairs when he takes a fancy to her."

Archambeau had regained his equilibrium. "Are we talking about the same man? A gentleman in his late thirties, with brown wavy hair, brown eyes, large ears, and a penchant for wearing ties of an alarming color?"

"Yes. Mysir Karl Solberg, who fancies himself an artist." She gave an audible sniff of disdain. "His work is nothing I can't buy along the canal from the weekend painters. I was once a model for a *real* artist, whose work was exhibited in the National Gallery."

The duke pressed for confirmation. "Perhaps he was simply talking with her regarding Lady Losendahl's business?"

"After they arrived, he met Hannah at the back door of the Royal that very evening. That was before he formally called on Lady Losendahl on Tuesday."

"What did you think of their relationship? New or ongoing?" I wondered.

"When you find Hannah, ask her. All I know is that the last day she was here, she consumed nothing but dry toast for breakfast and vomited it away in the chamberpot. And her with no ring on her finger!"

It was clear Madame Travers relished imparting that gossip to us, and the cruel but witty way she talked about others was fascinating. I could listen to her all day. She should be working for the newspapers as a gossip correspondent, not slaving away at the Royal.

"It looks like we have a lot to discuss with Mysir Solberg," said Archambeau.

"Indeed." Of Madame Travers I asked, "Is there anything else you specifically noticed about Lady Losendahl? Did she go out at all?"

"She left at 3 p.m. every day for a walking constitutional. Mys Wahl accompanied her. That took about an hour. Her only visitors were Mysir Solberg, and the two ladies who just left. On the last day, she changed her routine— I was correcting one of my silly girls in the hall when she walked by us at around eleven in the morning. Mys Wahl wasn't with her, and I thought that odd. It made me think her lover had finally agreed to a meeting."

"Did she give you anything?" I asked, thinking of the pearl necklace.

Madame Travers practically sneered. "I would refuse if she had. It's against the rules. But yes, she did give the maid who cleaned her room a set of very nice handkerchiefs. Linen with embroidered flowers at the corner. It was an expensive gift for only cleaning her room, and I told the girl to return them the next day, but Lady Losendahl never came back to the Royal, so she couldn't."

Archambeau had been taking in the conversation, but now spoke up. "And what of Mys Wahl's movements after Lady Losendahl's disappearance? How did she appear?"

"By dinner Mys Wahl was frantic, or so my maids told me. Practically wild, demanding if any of us had seen Mys Losendahl. Where had she gone? Had she left a note? Received any letters? Of course, she sent for Mysir Solberg and he was here for at least two hours with her sobbing all over his lapels." The sneer wasn't even hidden now, her contempt for Solberg obvious.

"But that wasn't when Mys Wahl left the hotel for good?" asked Archambeau.

"Oh no, Your Grace. She left the next morning, alone. In her best outfit and wearing new shoes. I noticed because they were two-tone, white with black lacing and edging. Far too fashionable for a lady's maid to be wearing. I imagine she stole them from Lady Losendahl's trunk."

It turned out that Baron Losendahl had escaped Stephan, the duke's secretary, for we found him with his daughter's things in her suite at the Royal Hotel. He had taken over Ebbe's suite upon his arrival, three days after her disappearance. That was fortunate for many reasons; searching what remained could give me more information about the missing woman.

"Did you learn anything?" asked the baron eagerly when we entered. His face was drawn with worry and he looked from me to the duke, begging for answers. Archambeau patted the shoulder of his friend.

I told him, "We have new information. A possible relationship Mysir Solberg may have been having with your daughter's maid. Did you suspect anything of that nature?"

From his flabbergasted expression, the answer was clear. "No, I did not."

His daughter's room was decorated tastefully in a very light gray-rose color scheme, with the chairs upholstered in a dark blue velvet. The windows looked out to the back courtyard and were framed with navy drapes edged with a ribbon of silver. There were several vases filled with fresh hothouse spring flowers on the mantle and the table, but I very much doubted the baron was in a state to appreciate their expensive beauty, though they would certainly be on his bill.

In the parlor there were no personal items. I put down my bag and announced, "I would like to see your daughter's jewel case. Do we need to send for it from the hotel safe?"

"No, I have it." He disappeared into what I presumed was one of the bedrooms and returned with a black velvet case.

Taking a seat, I opened it in my lap, and started searching through it. "There are not many items here of value. I would have expected more, since she was here to shop for a wedding trousseau."

The baron didn't seem surprised. "Ebbe said she'd worry about losing anything valuable on the train. Or having it stolen. She wasn't a girl for big pieces of jewelry."

"No earrings," I murmured. Closing it and setting it aside on the small table beside me, I brought out the string of Perino pearls from my pocket and held them up to him. "What can you tell me about these?"

For a large man, the baron could move quickly when he wanted. He was at my side instantly and took them gently from my hands, his eyes watering with emotion. "These were a gift from her mother. On her thirteenth birthday. I did not realize she had brought them with her."

"Well, then, I'm glad to return them to you. She gave them in trust to one of her friends, but that lady did not feel it right to keep them. Were there matching earrings? It looks like part of a set, but I do not find them here?"

"Yes, it was. The earrings had tiny diamonds set in a bow with a pearl drop." The baron still seemed stunned, his hands stroking the delicate necklace.

I asked gently, "Now, did she have a portable writing desk? I hear she wrote letters on a regular basis?"

It was fashionable for society ladies to keep a lap case to store their writing paper, wax and seals, as well as their inks for when they traveled. This, too, the baron brought me from the bedroom.

My hands slid smoothly over the expensive waxwood before I unlatched it. Opening the shallow, rectangular box, I got a whiff of ink, the deep rosin smell of the wood, and the scent of fine paper. Inside was only a set of pens, a glass bottle of jet ink, and blank sheets. No letters stored away that either Ebbe was in the process of writing, or that were sent to her. *Odd.*

Before I could state my suspicions that someone had been in the box before us, the door burst open and in spilled my assistant, Twyla Andricksson, followed by Inspector Marcellus Barbier of the gendarmes.

My protégé announced triumphantly, "We've found her! She's dead!"

Chapter Five

Grabbing Twyla under her arm, I told the room, "Excuse me." I shoved her into one of the bedrooms, closing the door behind us.

"What did you do that for?" the girl asked, rubbing her pinched arm.

"Be quiet and listen to what I'm about to say. If you open your mouth once more, I shall return you to the Morpheus Society in a locked trunk. Possibly in chopped up, bite-size pieces."

She opened her mouth to speak, and I slapped her. That stunned her enough to stop her chattering.

"I am not going to tell you again, Mys Andricksson. Shut your mouth and open your ears. I've put up with almost three months of you not obeying my instructions. Why? Because by contract I must accept any apprentice sent to me by the Morpheus Society at least once every ten years, and you were my first. But I won't hesitate to send you back, and pay the penalty for rejecting you."

Her eyes filled with angry tears, but at least she didn't say anything more. Furious, I was practically snarling in her face. "You don't have the least idea of what you've done! Barging in here and telling a father that his daughter is in the morgue is the worst news a parent could receive. Yet you show no compassion! Instead, you spill it in a gleeful, gloating manner. The damage is done. Now, will you keep silent as we go back into the other room?"

She nodded slowly, her eyes now showing doubt and hurt. Maybe I was getting through to her.

"You will not respond to anyone, only to me. Keep your answers short and to the questions I ask. Do you understand?" I turned my back on her and opened the door to return to the other room.

My reaction had been extreme, but this case involving a father and daughter was bringing back too many emotions. What I would give to have my own father returned to me! I was finding myself far too sympathetic with the baron's grief, and Twyla's childlike enthusiasm was grating sorely on old wounds.

Everyone ignored our return. Archambeau had his hand on the baron's shoulder while Losendahl hung his head, listening to the inspector. "...The age matches, and the hair color, but it would be best if you came down to identify her. Or would you prefer Solberg do that, your lordship?"

"No! I—" He looked up, and I could see that his eyes were filled with pain, unseeing. "I would prefer to do that. Can I do it now? I don't want to wait."

"Yes, we can if that suits you."

Baron Losendahl collected his hat and left with the inspector. To me, Archambeau said, avoiding Twyla's stare, "Grab your bag, Chalamet. We don't have a moment to lose if we wish to use your Ghost Talking talent."

Outside, as carriages were being arranged, Inspector Barbier told me, "Your apprentice is quite the firecracker."

"No chance I could send her to you, is there? She has expressed a love for detective work."

He grinned. "I could find her mounds of filing to do."

"I don't think that is the type of work she has in mind, although I might enjoy not seeing her for a while. But right now, I have a commitment to fulfill. How long has our body been dead? And what condition is it in?"

He stroked his long black mustache, thinking, his large brown eyes contemplative. "She's in one piece, but the face is beaten pretty badly. It will be touch and go if her father can identify her. Dr. LaRue should tell us more."

The inspector grabbed a quick-cab to take him to the mortuary, the rest of us following in the duke's carriage. None of us said anything during the ride. The baron held the string of his daughter's pearls in his hand like a talisman as he gazed blindly out the window. The somber mood in the carriage even impacted Twyla, for the girl worried her lip, shooting nervous glances between me and the baron.

The carriage made its way down Rue du Canal, rolling over one bridge, and then another. It took twenty minutes of silence to reach the university district, with its gray buildings and abandoned warehouses. As we passed the little restaurant where the duke had become possessed with the ghost of Bastiaan Hagen, I couldn't stop a faint smile from crossing my lips. When I looked across to Archambeau, he must have been thinking the same, for he gave me a slight half-smile.

The carriage clattered over the cobblestones and past the university gate to make a wide sweep along the back of the campus, to the morgue that was part of the medical teaching college. It was an area I was well acquainted with from my work with the gendarmes; it was also here that I had first met the Duke de Archambeau during the Giles Monet case.

When we stopped, the inspector was waiting for us, his hat held respectfully in his hands like an undertaker waiting for the family's arrival. Again, Archambeau helped me down the step, but ignored Twyla's outstretched hand. Well, she was young, she could jump down. She would not be forgiven soon by any of us for her misbehavior.

The inspector opened the back door of the brick building for the baron and the duke. "Right this way, your lordships."

Dr. LaRue was scrubbing blood off her hands and forearms when we entered. Under her apron she was dressed in men's trousers and vest, and the sleeves of her white shirt were rolled up to expose bony arms. She had cropped her hair to be level with her jawline in the new avant-garde style popular with the student set. It worked well with the angular shape of her face, throwing her bone structure in sharp relief.

She gave a nod of greeting to those she knew. "Your Grace, Elinor, Marcellus."

Archambeau introduced her to the baron, who was not paying attention, for his eyes were on the body lying on the table under a sheet. Guessing the reason for his presence, Charlotte said, "I've cleaned her up the best I can, but it's not a peaceful death. Brace yourself."

"I'm braced," croaked Baron Losendahl.

The sheet lifted.

"It's not Ebbe. It's Hannah Wahl!"

If a strong man could collapse, the baron was close to it. The duke pulled him away from the side of the corpse and forced him to sit down on a stool.

Hannah Wahl was pretty no more. Her face had been cruelly beaten, the nose broken, and one eye destroyed, and her throat had been slit. Her dress had been suggestively torn, and the white-and-black boots that Madame Travers had admired so much were dirty and scuffed.

"What do you know so far, Charlotte?" I asked.

Dr. LaRue re-covered the face of the girl, for which I was glad, and gave her report. "I haven't done the internal examination yet, but so far I know the beating took place shortly before her death. I don't think the damage was done by fists but by some sort of blunt object, probably wood, as I found a few splinters in her eye socket."

"A club? Bat?"

"More smooth than rough. She was on the ground at some point, for there are bruises on the ribcage and thighs, probably from someone kicking her. Death from a very sharp knife used across the throat. It almost decapitated her."

I turned away to stare at the wall. I'd seen some pretty horrific deaths in my years of assisting the police, but this one was hard to stomach.

"She was last seen five days ago," Archambeau said.

"Dead soon after that, I'd imagine."

"Who found her?"

Charlotte nodded behind me to where Sergeant Dupont stood stolidly against the wall, near the door. While a big man, girth making him round as an egg, he was a quiet one and thus easy to miss. "That girl of yours, Andricksson, found her first and then took Dupont to the body."

Before I could ask any more questions, the baron, who was evidently still recovering from the shock, demanded, "My daughter! Where is she?!"

"I believe Madame Chalamet may be able to help us," suggested Archambeau. "What do you think, Elinor? Can you?"

"Certainly I can try a Ghost Talk. But remember, it has limitations."

Shooting a glance at his friend, Archambeau said, "You must try."

"Another possibility is that if her soul has already transitioned to the Afterlife, we can try the area where she was found for haunted residue."

"Was she killed where she was found?" asked Archambeau.

"Seems to have been, from Sergeant Dupont's report," said Inspector Barbier, consulting his notebook. "It was a back alley in the Hells, the only place someone could leave a body undisturbed for five days. And there was a pool of blood around her."

Twyla finally spoke up. "The earrings. Why didn't someone steal them?"

"Actually, she's only wearing one," said Charlotte. "The other earlobe shows a tear. Probably it was lost during the beating. She does have defensive wounds on her hands and skin under her nails. She fought back, but it wasn't much use, poor thing."

Archambeau asked, "Was the other earring found in the alley?"

"Not yet," said Barbier. "But I'll send Sergeant Dupont to search again. Who knows what might be concealed in the alley's refuse?"

At least Twyla was well briefed on how to set up a Ghost Talking session. She took out the brazier from my valise, placed a coal inside it, and lit it. Leaving her to that, I used my vial of Eyesbright, placing several drops in my eyes. The room changed from my normal vision to a hazy purple-silver.

"Yes, that packet." I nodded at the one Twyla had chosen. She set it on the hot coal, and it started to smoke. Breathing in the scent, I handed the bottle of Eyesbright to the girl. "Use it."

The smoke was growing thicker, and with it light-headedness set in. Soon I would be able to collect what memories of Hannah Wahl remained after her murder.

Taking Twyla's hand in a fierce grip so she couldn't let go, I told her, "The dead you have worked with before passed peacefully from illness or natural causes. Our mentor, Madame Granger, showed you the gentle side of death. Now you shall see another face."

Ghost Talking wasn't a séance, though it is easy to confuse the two. In Ghost Talking, you were viewing impressions left in the body from when it had walked the earth. In a séance, you were actually summoning a spirit from the Beyond that had not transitioned.

Unlike with Giles Monet, there was nothing here bound to the corporal. Sending a summoning to the Beyond for Hannah Wahls' spirit also yielded nothing. She must have transitioned quickly to the Afterlife. The third option was to search for the living echo of her existence on the earthly plan.

Placing my hand on the sheet, I felt the corpse underneath. Using that to anchor me, I searched for any memory that her existence might have left behind in Alenbonné. Bringing those patchwork images together, I sorted them like a puzzle. Gathering them inside my heart, feeding them energy from myself and my protégé, I formed pictures for the others to see.

Twyla gasped, crying. "It hurts! Make it stop!"

During a Ghost Talk, a medium took on the emotional pain of the death, and while the intensity of it might fade over time, it would always leave small cuts upon your heart that never healed. My apprentice was learning what it truly meant to commune with the dead. This day, Twyla Andricksson would be changed forever, as I had once been.

I blew upon a dying coal, coaxing memories to life. In a moment, Hannah's energy residue of her earthly footprint would be revealed.

"That's Ebbe! Our Ebbe!" cried the baron as I materialized the image of his daughter handing a pair of earrings to her maid, Hannah Wahl. Well, at least I was able to clear the girl of the accusation of theft. Small comfort.

Scenes faded in and out of a man about my age. Karl Solberg? He matched the duke's description: brown wavy hair, large ears. He had a receding chin and his brown eyes showed a weakness of character.

I spoke aloud for the first time. "This is the most recent memory I can find."

Flickering into being, Hannah received a note, but we couldn't read it. After grabbing her hat, she rushed from the Royal Hotel and hailed a quick-cab. In a dark alley, we saw her walking up to a man wearing a dark blue coat. He was wearing a hat with a domed crown like someone of the working class.

That was all I could retrieve of her life, for her soul's print on our earthly plan was so light, so insubstantial, that I could gather nothing else from the last week of the girl's life. As I opened my eyes, I shook off the spell of being in the Beyond, dropping Twyla's hand.

"Why couldn't we question her? Like Giles Monet's shade?" asked the duke.

"She's transitioned to the Afterlife, while Monet was still trapped in the Beyond by the ghost dragon. The only thing I could access is the earth's memory of her time here and even that is beginning to fade."

"Is this what a Ghost Talker does?" asked Baron Losendahl. His face showed surprise and wonder as he stared at where the images had appeared on the morgue wall.

"This is what Madame Elinor Chalamet does," said Archambeau, rather proudly.

Meanwhile, Twyla, still shaking from what she had experienced, whispered hoarsely, "I didn't know."

I brought her into a reassuring embrace so I could whisper into her ear, "Now you do. So respect the dead and their loved ones, alright?"

She nodded against my shoulder, which was becoming a bit damp with tears.

"How did you find Hannah, Twyla?"

She sniffled, "That street boy, Marcus, showed up at your rooms. He wanted to know if you had any work for him, and I asked him if it would be possible for him to ask all the newsboys throughout Alenbonné if anyone knew about a young lady new to the neighborhood who didn't belong there. I thought maybe Mys Wahl or Lady Losendahl took a room in a boarding house. I was thinking she had run off, you see."

The newsboys were everywhere, saw everything, and brushed

elbows with the high and low. Marcus, my street rat, would know them all. It was a good idea.

"That was very clever of you about the newsboys, Twyla, but please, next time, don't go into the Hells without a guardia. It's not something even I would do."

"Well, when I found her, I did go back with a guardia! With him." Her thumb rather rudely pointed to Sergeant Dupont. "Inspector Barbier was too busy to help. He said I would be safe with him, even though he does seem as thick as a rack of mutton."

Sergeant Dupont might as well have been an automaton— one of those new carnival machines that didn't move unless you dropped a Royal coin inside the slot— for he made no response to this. But he was big and imposing, with a nightstick at his side, as well as a pair of come-alongs hanging from his belt.

Over her head, I asked the inspector, "Will you take Mys Andricksson back to her hostel? She needs rest for now."

The inspector cleared his throat, bringing our attention to him. "I'll have Dupont drop her off before I send him back to search where Wahl was found. Perhaps we can find that other earring or more evidence."

After Barbier, Dupont, and Twyla left to arrange cabs, the baron addressed me and the duke. "Now what do we do?"

"Mysir Karl Solberg is overdue for another visit," said Archambeau.

Chapter Six

The duke and baron left for the courtyard, but I hung back. At my request, Charlotte wrapped the pearl earring in some cotton gauze and gave it to me.

I asked quietly, "By the way, Charlotte, was Mys Wahl pregnant?"

Her prominent brown eyes sparkled with interest. "I haven't done the organs yet. Do you want to wait here while I find out?"

"No, thank you. But could you send me a message? To the Crown when you know, yes or no?"

"Certainly."

In the courtyard, Twyla and Sergeant Dupont were gone and Inspector Barbier was asking details about Ebbe Losendahl's disappearance from her father, jotting it all down in his notebook. With the evidence of a crime, he was now taking the baron seriously.

After a Ghost Talk like that one, I wasn't surprised to feel a bit of a headache forming behind my eyes, which were still seeing purple hues on the edge of my vision. The heavy weight on my heart after taking on the burden of yet another murdered person made for a sad ache in my bones.

Never mind that this entire case reminded me too much of my

father's murder. The desperation and grief of wanting to know what happened was mirrored afresh by the presence of the baron. The crime of a callous murder of a young girl, her throat cut, as had been my father's. Then there was the mischief someone with the Morpheus Society was possibly doing that was still needing an investigation.

As if he read my dark thoughts, Archambeau walked over and asked quietly, "How are you holding up, Chalamet?"

"Nothing I can't handle."

"I noticed Mys Andricksson seems unduly distressed."

"She'll adapt, like we all do."

"Usually I'm the one who is accused of being harsh with my subordinates, Chalamet. Will the girl be all right?"

The headache made me reply sharply. "She should have counted the cost before bragging about wanting to detect crime!"

"The cost? What is the cost?" he pressed. "I want to know what you mean, and you are equally determined not to tell me. Why won't you tell me?"

"Since you wish to know, when a medium Ghost Talks, we take on a soul's grief at being untimely torn from the world."

I could feel his gaze on me, but I kept my eyes staring forward. Kindness and sympathy would break me. After a long moment, he said, "Sometimes I sense a heaviness in you, Elinor. I thought that due to your father's death."

For one second, our eyes met. Feeling vulnerable, I replied softly, "We all bear scars. Some not visible."

Our conversation was cut short, for the baron was growing impatient. Already in the duke's carriage, he leaned out the window to address us. "Are we to wait here all day? If Solberg hid something from us, I shall wring it all out of him this time."

Archambeau held the door for me. As I clambered in, I asked Barbier over my shoulder, "Are you coming with us, then?"

"Yes, for it's a criminal matter now."

After the duke, the inspector gripped the door frame and

quickly stepped inside, holding his lame leg stiffly out as he took a seat beside me. In a moment we were off, rolling across the city, back to where Solberg had lodgings.

With information from his sister, we found Mysir Karl Solberg on Rue du Canal, where he had his easel set up for an afternoon of painting. In one thing, Madame Travers was correct: his work was mediocre. He was very charming, though— disgustingly charming, and completely oblivious to the dark mood of our little company.

"Baron Losendahl, Duke de Archambeau, I hope you have located our wayward girls?" he said gaily, waving a paint brush at us.

The baron's expression might have been why Archambeau stepped forward to put himself between the two men.

"No, we have not," the duke said calmly. "Let me introduce you to Inspector Marcellus Barbier of the gendarmes and Madame Elinor Chalamet. They are helping us in trying to locate Lady Losendahl."

"Oh, is that so?" Solberg babbled. He started hastily to clean his brushes with turpentine, wiping them across a cloth stained with many colors.

"We were lucky enough to locate Hannah Wahl, her maid," said Barbier coolly. Perhaps something in that alerted the rabbit, for he visibly started, before returning his oils, brushes, and palette in his porchade, his portable work box.

"If anyone knows where Ebbe is, I'm sure it would be Hannah." His head bobbed at his own statement.

The duke and baron moved to either side of the gentleman artist, boxing him in. The move made him nervous, and he fumbled with the latch to close the art box.

He mumbled, "The spring light is so troublesome. Not bright

enough in the late afternoon to make decent work. I think it's best that I quit for the day."

Archambeau said coldly, "I do not think Mys Wahl will be telling us anything. She is lying in the city morgue."

The box dropped from Mysir Solberg's hand, hitting the pavement. One of the cheap hinges broke and it opened, scattering his tools of the trade across the walking path. He scrambled to his knees, trying to get all of his brushes and paints together.

Nervous tell, or useful distraction?

The baron grabbed one arm, the duke the other. Picking him up, they literally carried him to a park bench. The inspector hid a smile behind his notepad. With the two men solid as bookends on either side of their victim, Barbier started asking questions, his words a rapid staccato.

"When was the last time you saw Mys Wahl?"

"I-I told these two gentlemen already. She sent me a note last Wednesday. Sh-sh-she was very upset that Lady Losendahl had not returned. I came as soon as I could get away."

"Away from what?"

"My mother's. It was well after luncheon when I got the note."

"But that wasn't the first time you saw Mys Wahl." Archambeau's smile was one a cat made before it broke the back of the mouse it was playing with.

"Y-y-yes, I saw Hannah with Ebbe on Tuesday. The day after they arrived."

His attempt to stand up earned him a shove back down by the baron. It was so forceful that his heels flew up from the ground. If Solberg escaped this conversation without being beaten, it would be a close call; Baron Losendahl wanted to pound out his frustration, and Solberg would be a satisfying target.

Archambeau said, examining his nails, his eyes watching Solberg through his lashes, "We know you lied to us, Solberg. You met Mys Wahl the first evening she arrived. We have a witness, so don't try telling us another fairy story."

Solberg gaped like a fish. Glug, glug, glug went his opened mouth. After the third gobble, he said, "Yes. Yes, I did meet Hannah that evening. I wanted to see Ebbe, but she had already retired because of being tired from the train trip."

Baron Losendahl erupted. Lightning fast, his fist boxed Solberg's right ear. The force of it sent the man cringing down on the bench, clutching his head.

The baron loomed over him as he shouted, "No more stories! We know what your relationship was with Hannah. That you deceived me and my wife about your intentions to our daughter to hide your affair with a maidservant. If we were in Zulskaya, I would hitch you to the back of my sled and drag you over the mountains until your bones rattled off all your flesh."

Inspector Barbier twirled his pencil in one hand. "Now, let's not talk about dragging or beatings in front of the law. Perhaps, though, Mysir Solberg, it would be best to be honest at this point in our interview?"

I took Karl Solberg to be one of those men to whom lies came easily; the truth, not so much. It would take him time to remember it, and the rising fist of the baron getting ready to box his other ear wasn't helping. The grim faces of the other two men weren't giving him any peace of mind, either. Perhaps a woman's touch was needed.

"Mysir Solberg, I would greatly like to know more about when you first met Ebbe Losendahl."

"What do you mean?"

"What did you think of her? What did the two of you discuss during those long walks?"

He gave the baron a fearful glance.

"Don't worry, you can speak freely to me. The duke won't let Ebbe's father smash you to a pulp if you answer my questions. If you don't care to speak, though, I can make no such guarantee."

He gulped and wiped his forehead with his paint rag, leaving a streak of cobalt blue over his forehead. "W-well, she was pretty.

Not as pretty as Hannah, of course. But she had a way of talking to you, asking questions, that made you think she was hanging on every word you said. Quite flattering it was, to have such attention."

"But your attention wandered to her maid?"

Another fearful glance at the baron. "Ebbe was as snowy as her mountains. She froze me out. No kisses allowed. No encouragement. She'd barely let me hold her hand!"

There was such a mad glitter in Baron Losendahl's eyes that Archambeau had to put out a hand to physically restrain him from moving forward to grab Solberg by his paint-stained lapels.

"Tsk-tsk. Not affectionate, then? No wonder your courtship didn't flourish."

"See, you understand! She shut me down anytime I tried to stroke her hair or go in for a cuddle. Hannah was more willing and prettier. I mean, I am only a man!"

"So, what did you two talk about? What drew Lady Losendahl's attention to you in the first place?"

He scratched his unhurt ear. There was a flake of drying paint on it that was most likely itching. "That Morpheus Society stuff. She loved hearing about their little parties."

"Parties?"

"It's all hush-hush. The invite is sent anonymously to a select few. People who would be interested in that sort of thing." He giggled. Actually giggled! "All the men come in a black domino with a matching mask. The girls wear white gowns and white masks."

"What does this have to do with the Morpheus Society?" I asked, befuddled.

"They run it. They use a girl, called the Chosen One, as the medium, and she makes dozens of ghosts appear all at the same time. Ghosts that appear as solid as you or I."

This did not sound good.

"Tell us all about it," said Archambeau, his voice vibrating with the strength it took to control his anger. I was too appalled to speak.

Solberg started babbling again, happy to tell us something that was less personal than an affair with a servant girl. "It's held every full moon. There's a ceremony where we stand in two circles. The inner circle is all the girls, and the outer circle is the men. In the center is the Chosen One, the living made dead. She lies down on a divan and after she drinks from a cup, falls asleep as if dead. Then all the spirits appear. Once they materialize, you can touch them like real people. Some guests dance with them, play cards, kiss them, or— you know— do other things with them in private rooms."

"That — is — not — possible!" I exclaimed.

He shrugged. "I'm telling you what I saw. They seem to be as real as you or me, but I know for a fact they're dead. One of them was a man I knew who was killed in a carriage accident about four years ago."

Ignoring my shocked expression, the duke asked, "What happens to the Chosen One? When the party ends?"

"Not sure. She never wakes up during the party. At one point I sneaked over and pinched her really hard, but she didn't react at all."

This really did not sound good.

Chapter Seven

Karl Solberg knew little more about the ghost entertainments, as he had attended only two. He had been directed to meet at a central point, at a statue in Fontaine Park, near the mermaid statue. There he had been blindfolded and transported by carriage with a ride that could have been ten minutes or half an hour.

"When we got there, I remember going down steps."

"Anything else?" asked Archambeau, clearly growing impatient with our artist.

Inside, the blindfold was removed. He described where the parties were held, which did not sound familiar to any of us: a large, open interior area that sounded like a warehouse of some sort.

"What happens at the end? To the young ladies in this ritual?" the baron demanded. His hand spasmed before he clasped it hard behind his back with his other, presumably in order to physically restrain himself from strangling the man.

"I don't know! I really don't. At the end, we left as we came in. As far as I know, the Chosen One wakes up, but it doesn't happen during the party."

"Was the floor pavement or wood?" asked Archambeau.

"Stone. I remember it being cold and wishing they'd have a brazier lit or something, but they had only torches held by brackets on the wall."

"Were the walls also stone? Or plaster?"

"Stone. Not like man-made bricks, but like quarried stone. Dark gray."

"Were the walls damp?"

"I don't remember."

"Was there a smell?"

"Yes. A bit moldy."

"Now tell me more about how you got the invitation. And was this the only party you attended?" ended Archambeau.

He looked nervously at where the men were standing. "I've been twice. I think I got the first invitation because I attended a lecture at the Hall of Science about spirits that the Morpheus Society was holding. It's the only time I've had anything to do with the Society, so that's how I figured they became aware of my interest. They make you sign a guest book before you enter the lecture hall."

"But why do you think the Society is hosting the party? From what you have described, no one seems to take credit."

"I don't remember who, but someone told me the Society was doing the parties," he stubbornly maintained.

When it seemed we had drained him of all knowledge, we let him go. The sun was starting to set and, at the baron's insistence, we four adjourned to a private dining room at the Royal Hotel to discuss what we had learned. Settled around the round table with its white tablecloth, silver, and crystal, we began our council of war.

"So these parties are a complete surprise to you?" asked Archambeau as he snapped open a cloth napkin to place in his lap.

"I've never heard of them! I cannot believe these things are endorsed by the Morpheus Society," I said firmly, despite a doubt in the back of my mind.

The duke, his gaze going around the table, said, "Two days ago, I went to the Morpheus Society's Persephone Club and spoke with Parnell Lafayette. He said he knew nothing about Ebbe Losendahl and when pressed, grew angry."

"Mysir Lafayette is an easy person to anger," I said.

"You have experience with him?"

"Yes, he trained as a Ghost Talker about twelve years ago. He is very arrogant and conceited, nor does he take kindly to anyone challenging him. And while I am sure you were diplomatic, Your Grace—"

"You are too kind, Chalamet. I was not diplomatic. Suffice it to say that our personalities did not mix well together."

"You should have come to me first," I told him, causing the baron to speak up.

"I wanted to keep things quiet and thought we would locate Ebbe quickly enough. That was due to my reticence, I'm afraid. How wrong I was."

The dinner arrived, and so did Sergeant Dupont and Twyla. She had disobeyed my order and had gone with the sergeant to the Hells to search for the earring. Perhaps I would have been angry with her, but she looked drained and exhausted as she took a seat next to my own.

She murmured to me, "I'm sorry, madame, but I had to try to find it."

"We shall discuss that later," I responded, not having the heart to chastise her any more.

The inspector finished taking Dupont's report, which was mostly one-word mumbles; the sergeant left just as the first course arrived. After the servers had departed and with the door closed, Archambeau asked the room, "Have you had any girls reported missing, Inspector?"

He cut into his fish. "My department rarely gets le beau idéal seeking my help, Your Grace, unless it's about a servant whom they believe has committed a theft. They do not bring their family problems to us."

There was an uncomfortable silence, though no one pointed it out that the baron had told him about Ebbe, and Barbier had ignored him.

Perhaps he felt the sting of our thoughts, for Barbier said defensively, "If you don't mind me saying, these parties sound like an entertainment fueled by drugs and alcohol to me. A stage show for the rubes. Something a variety show magician would put together. A circus act."

"So you've heard of no disappearances? Strange runaways? Nothing of that sort?" persisted Archambeau.

"With this new information, I'll review the reports over the last few months at the station, but I'd swear the first young woman Dr. LaRue has had in her surgery since midwinter was the one we saw today."

While generally not squeamish, I did not want to think about where the body of Hannah Wahl was right now as I stared down at my plate.

"What parties?" asked Twyla, who had been revived by food and wine. Spirit work depleted the body, and we needed food to replace the energy drained by it. I would need to remind her to care for herself; it would be easy for a person like Twyla, who did not pay attention to details, to become run-down and weak.

I brought her up to date on what we had learned from Mysir Solberg. "Have you ever heard of any such thing?"

Twyla had a habit of scrunching her nose when thinking, and it made you aware of her freckles on her cheeks. "Not anything about that, but there do seem to be more requests for training coming from young women. No one above thirty, as far as I could tell. The class forming when I left was almost all girls— no men at all, or even older people like you'd expect."

"Why older people?" asked the baron curiously.

"The closer you are to death, the more you want to know," I told him. To Twyla, I asked, "Nothing was said by Mysir Lafayette or Madame Granger about some new method to reach the Beyond? Or some different way to materialize ghosts?"

"Mysir Lafayette is working on some hush-hush project."

"Now, that sounds promising," said the duke. "What do you know of it?"

Twyla blossomed under his noble interest. "Oh, he was so jealous when Madame Chalamet's paper about that ghost dragon was submitted to the committee for review! He ranted up and down the halls for days, but then he locked himself away and all got quiet. That all happened right before I was sent to apprentice under Madame Chalamet, so unfortunately I don't know more."

The baron asked the group, "What is this Morpheus Society? Is it part of the university? The government?"

I answered. "We are not a government entity, but a private society of amateurs determined to examine the soul's journey after death— what we often call the supernatural. We were founded by Lady Alouette Sarte, who set out the guidelines of how to examine the three planes of existence as scientifically as the field of medicine does the human body."

"So... an educational group?"

"Yes, but independent of the university and funded through philanthropy and by member dues. To be accepted, a mentor must agree to guide you, like Madame Granger did me back when I wanted to join. Later, students spend a year or two taking educational lectures from other members before they are certified as a full member of the Society."

"So this is where mediums come from?"

Thinking of Madame Nyght, I said firmly, "Not all mediums are from the Society. It is best to inquire and make sure they are endorsed by us."

"We have thirty-two practitioners right now," said Twyla proudly.

Archambeau was surprised. "I don't recall seeing so many when I was researching the matter in the Nyght case."

"Most of those that begin training drop out for one reason or another. And many of those who finish don't do public service like madame does," said Twyla, who was gobbling down her food too quickly. Her table manners would need improvement. Another thing to speak to her about. Having an apprentice was exhausting!

With Twyla's mouth full, I returned to explaining. "Most start the training out of curiosity and once they realize the real work it takes to become accomplished enough to succeed on a consistent basis, they decide the effort it would take is not worth it. Others hope to contact a dead loved one, and once that task is completed, they abandon their studies. I only joined after Inspector Barbier suggested it to me as a way I could contact my dead father."

The inspector nodded. "I was a sergeant at the time, working on the team investigating Augustus Chalamet's death when I met Elinor. When our leads dwindled to nothing, I thought Madame Granger with the Society could help. But I never thought Elinor would actually become a Ghost Talker herself. Or provide our department with assistance to solve cases."

I smiled his way, letting him see my thanks for his care of me, before taking up my story. "Yes, unfortunately the Society was unable to help me. My father had transitioned to the Afterlife, and no one can breach that mystery, not even a Ghost Talker. But the idea of speaking with spirits fascinated me, and I decided to continue with it."

"But you weren't any good at it. Not like me. I'm a natural, Madame Granger says so!" Twyla bragged.

The girl truly had no awareness of the insults that came out of her mouth. Shaking my head, I tried to be lighthearted about it. "Mys Andricksson is right. I wasn't any good. It was like swimming through mud. All uphill work, with many midnight candles burned before I started seeing success."

"Hard work pays off," said Archambeau, his frowning countenance chastising my apprentice.

Undaunted by his rebuke, Twyla said cheerfully, "Oh, I know it does! Madame Granger told me I would learn a lot from Madame Chalamet."

"I'm sure she did! Perhaps she hoped I would be able to teach you restraint."

"Who is this Madame Granger?" asked the baron. "You've mentioned her several times."

"She was my mentor when I entered the Society. It was her good hands that shaped me into the Ghost Talker I am today."

"So the Morpheus Society uses an apprentice arrangement?"

"First, you must be sponsored to join the group. Techniques you learn in classes and with lectures, but skill you must hone under someone who has agreed to teach you. Later, after graduating from the Society, you apprentice for about a year."

Archambeau mused, "That could explain who Lady Losendahl was waiting for when she reached town. A mentor. Someone who had promised to take her on, either with the Society's knowledge of the arrangement or not."

"Her correspondence case was empty of any letters— received or in the progress of being written," I pointed out. "That seems unusual for a woman who was taught to write weekly letters to all her school chums. Either she or someone else destroyed them."

Archambeau replied, "We need to find out who was her contact with the Society. Mysir Solberg does not seem to know, and if Mys Wahl did, that is now lost with her."

I explained to the baron, "I wish the Ghost Talking had gained us more information, but Mys Wahl had transitioned to the Afterlife, and there is little to be gained from the body we leave behind."

Baron Losendahl asked, "Ghost Talking? That is what you call it? I've never seen anything like it before. If you had asked me if it could be done, I'd say it was smoke and mirrors."

"As I have thought in the past," agreed Archambeau. "But

Madame Chalamet is no fraud, Viktor. If anyone can help us with this matter, I'm sure it will be her."

I actually blushed. High praise indeed. "What I suggest is that I visit with Madame Granger and find out what she may know about these parties or if she heard anything about Lady Losendahl."

Inspector Barbier had finished his meal and was now jotting down notes in his moleskin notebook. I asked him, "This strange location that Mysir Solberg spoke of. I wonder if we can locate it?"

He gave me a bit of a smirk, flipping his notebook closed. "Already listed, Elinor. Along with getting that guest book from the Hall of Science. That would give us a list of names of those who might have also received invitations."

We all made arrangements about what we would do the next day, and our party broke up. Inspector Barbier was the first to leave, shaking hands with the men and giving Twyla and me a tip of the bowler hat in goodbye.

Since Baron Losendahl was staying at the Royal, he simply bade us all a good night. He would spend tomorrow morning going through a series of letters his wife had sent on that were from his daughter's room and see if they had any new information, perhaps a hint of a name we could pursue.

"What about me?" Twyla asked eagerly as I pulled on my gloves.

"I'd like you to review the newspapers over the last six months, with attention paid to the agony and the personal column. Advertisements looking for wayward daughters and lost housemaids." At her pout, I added, "If you prefer not to do this research, I shall send Anne-Marie, and you can do her cleaning and dusting!"

"Oh, all right," she said sulkily.

In the lobby, Twyla was sent off in a quick-cab back to her hostel for young ladies. Before I could call one for myself, the duke asked, "I'll take you back in my carriage, if you don't mind, Chalamet?"

"Certainly," I agreed, trying to appear nonchalant.

Chapter Eight

The carriage was traveling parallel to the canal, and the light from the waxing moon made the water silver.

"Where are we going, Your Grace? The Crown is only a few blocks from the Royal, and this is in the opposite direction."

"Just a round through the park so we can discuss the case. We haven't had a private moment since we met."

Nice that he would finally acknowledge that! Indeed, the last time we had been private was at Lindengaard when he was about to kiss me before Twyla's appearance interrupted us. That seemed a long time ago now.

Upon his unexpected arrival outside of Madame Chappelle's home after the séance, I had expected some sign of warmth or amiability from him, but he'd seemed focused only upon the case, treating me as an ally, only a bit better than Barbier. While I pride myself upon my professionalism, and appreciated it in others, surely the man was not this dense? Wasn't our relationship on some other level than merely colleagues?

"I thought you would like an update about King Guénard, since we haven't seen each other since the Winter Revels. He's recovered from his poisoning, and his doctor seems pleased with his progress. King Guénard greatly appreciates what you and your friend did for him."

I had no interest in discussing the king.

"Charlotte greatly appreciates her bank account balance," I replied cynically.

"His Majesty wants to know what reward would please you."

Perhaps I should have been grateful, but my irritation with Archambeau was growing. My tone was acerbic. "For now, I will keep King Guénard's gratitude on account to be drawn upon later. Charlotte was foolish to jump at mere money. She should have held out for something more meaningful."

"Such as?"

My mind leapt to all sorts of things, but I didn't voice any of them. "I'm sure I'll think of something when the right time presents itself." It seemed that if I wanted some explanation for his silence these last few months, I would have to ask. Well, he had said that we didn't play by society's rules. "What have you been doing? Working for His Majesty?"

From his position of leaning forward over his knees, he retreated, crossing his arms, his manner becoming withdrawn. "Yes."

So informative! I couldn't understand him. At times confiding, sharing details about his dead wife, asking after my welfare, and the next saying nothing that he couldn't broadcast to the world. I found his manner confusing, and things that puzzled me I wanted solved, even if I had to break them open with a hammer.

"He seems to keep you busy."

"Yes."

I threw my hands up in the air and rolled my eyes.

"What?" he asked.

"*What?*" I mimicked. "You vanish from my life, and return as if nothing has happened in the meantime!"

"The work I do for His Majesty is confidential. I cannot discuss it."

Now I crossed my arms. "That is the favor that I ask from His Majesty, then. Tell me what you have been working on. Where have you been?"

"You think my secrets are worth as much as a lifetime annuity? You value my knowledge highly, Elinor. I would hold out for the money. It's a dividend that pays far better."

I lifted my chin. "So you will not grant my wish for saving the king's life?"

"Technically, I think it was Dr. LaRue who saved his life, but I won't quibble. What I do is dirty work. Not something I would normally discuss with a lady, even if I had the king's permission."

"I just saw a dead girl who had her head hanging on by a thread. Don't talk to me about dirty work."

Strangely, he expelled a breath he was holding in a silent laugh. "You've made your point. However, without His Majesty's express permission, I can speak only in general terms. Still, you must promise not to repeat what I tell you to anyone. To apprentice or to the gendarmes."

"'Strictly confidential' is my motto."

"Hm. Since you already hold a secret about His Majesty, I think you are a safe risk, as much as one can be." There was a pregnant pause. "For the last few months, I've been hunting a monster throughout Sarnesse. It has many tentacles and affects every level of society, spreading corruption everywhere."

"What do you mean?"

"Money, stolen goods, drugs, prostitution. It is the largest criminal network I've ever encountered and has spread far, even to our neighbors, Perino and Zulskaya. As soon as I cut off one arm, I discover three others. It has kept me busy, with no time for social calls upon an intriguing, but vexing, lady."

Flattery soothed some of my harsher feelings toward him. His intriguing problem did the rest. "Does Inspector Barbier know? Are you working with him?"

Archambeau shook his head. "No, and do not speak of it to him or anyone. It involves people at the highest level, both in government and among the nobility."

"Do you think Lady Ebbe's disappearance is a part of this criminal enterprise?"

"Perhaps. It is why I want you to be especially careful. The savagery of Hannah Wahl's murder points to more than just mumbo-jumbo with ghosts. Perhaps Mys Wahl knew the identity of Lady Ebbe's mentor and was killed because of it."

"That seems logical," I agreed. "However, the brutality of the attack seems to suggest someone very adept with the use of violence. And what of the earring? Why take only one? Are we to believe those in the Hells so squeamish or delicate in their feelings that they would not pick over Hannah's body? Reselling her boots alone would probably keep a family in food for several months."

"Perhaps they knew her killer and didn't want to disturb his handiwork?"

"Perhaps."

His next question made my back stiffen again. "You honestly don't know anything about these parties?"

"I thought you trusted me? Of course I do not!"

"No hint? Perhaps you've heard something and forgot it?"

I said sarcastically, "I'd remember it if someone mentioned a séance where ghosts danced and kissed living people. It's not something I'd soon forget."

"It would only be natural if you wanted to protect the Morpheus Society."

"Why? Do you think I am sentimental? Blindingly loyal?" He was making me angry all over again.

"No. Of course not! But they did take you in after the murder of your father. You might feel protective towards such people."

"Not to the cost of a woman's life, I would not," I said firmly, hoping he would drop the subject.

The Duke de Archambeau wasn't a man who danced lightly when he wanted information. "But you had a mentor? When you joined? This Granger woman."

"Yes. Mentors do have a great deal of influence over their students. A very close bond is formed, since we examine death and grieving for our work. However, I do not see how Ebbe Losendahl, in a matter of a few days, would feel so strongly for someone as to leave her family forever."

"What if she was promised something she always wanted that only they could provide?"

It was not hard to see what he was implying. "You mean to be reunited with her lost friend, Labrenda Elstad?"

He nodded. "What would you sacrifice to speak again with your father?"

I did not answer, but he must have seen my agitation, for he changed seats and took one of my gloved hands in his own.

"I know you miss him dearly, Elinor. If you can use my help with your investigation into his death, ask me."

"Thank you. It's been hard."

As his carriage rolled to a stop in front of the Crown Hotel, I began to tell him, finally tell someone, about the vision my father's watch had given me. "When I was at your townhome, I was given back his watch—"

Someone fumbled at the carriage door and a drunk Jacques Moreau cried out, "I thought this coat of arms was the Duke de Archambeau's. Are you in there, Elinor? I've won at least one hundred crowns. Come and help me celebrate!"

His face was pressed against the carriage window, fogging the glass. With a muttered exclamation, I stepped out of the carriage. Standing there, I looked back to the carriage interior where Archambeau's face revealed a fleeting look of disgust and irritation at Jacques. He gave me a curt goodbye before calling up to his coachmen to take him home.

Jacques was in a condition described as standing-up-drunk. His smile was lopsided and his eyes a bit misty, but he could carry on a conversation. "A hundred crowns! Imagine that! Let's go to the theater. Or the opera. You choose."

There are certain things a lady can't say in public. Standing at the curb of the Crown hotel, I tried to be polite. "No thank you. I've got other plans."

Raising my hand, I gestured to a quick-cab parked on the other side of the street. Though it was late evening, I felt my errand could not wait. Besides, I wanted to get away from Jacques, and if I went into the Crown he would follow me.

The driver turned his horse around and headed in my direction. While I waited, tapping a foot, Jacques said mournfully, "You never have time for me anymore, Elinor. Why is that?"

"Jacques, I'm busy," I told him, trying to shake him off.

I handed up a folded bill to the driver and gave the address of Madame Leona Granger's house. She kept late hours, and I hoped to ask her about Lafayette. Archambeau implying I would excuse the Morpheus Society of ill-doing had stung; I wanted answers and would pursue them immediately.

Before I could close the door flap over my knees, Jacques jumped in, rocking the cab with his weight as he sat beside me. He put his arm around my shoulders and leaned in close. "Where are you off to in such a hurry?"

My gloved hand shoved his face away. "You reek of tobacco and alcohol."

He laughed, but retreated to his side. "Where are we going?"

"I'm going to a friend's home. When we get there, you can go back to the barracks."

"That isn't friendly."

Perhaps if I hadn't been in the middle of an investigation,

trying to find a woman before she was drugged or worse, I would have found Jacques' antics amusing. Or would I?

Even soused, my unhappiness with him finally sank into his thick head. He became apologetic. "I really didn't mean to upset you, Elinor. Just thought you'd want some fun on my last evening here in Alenbonné."

Oh my, was it his last day? With the problem of the missing Ebbe, I had completely lost track of time. I felt guilty and said lamely, "I didn't realize the date."

"Reporting for duty tomorrow, and then off with Axe to patrol the provinces." Axe was General Somerville, Jacques' commanding officer and whom he worked for as secretary. They'd probably be gone until fall.

I reached out and patted his hand. "I'm truly sorry, Jacques, but I'm working on an investigation for the Duke de Archambeau."

He crossed his arms, settling his chin on his chest as he extended his long legs. His boot heels rapped hard against the front interior of the quick-cab as he stamped them, almost like a toddler having a tantrum. "Didn't I warn you about him? Stay away from the man, Elinor."

Sympathy gone, I snapped, "You are not my father, Jacques."

"Honorary big brother, though, aren't I?"

"You've been telling me what to do since I was knee-high, but if you haven't noticed, I've grown up since then. I can manage my own affairs, thank you very much."

"And I'm still looking after you," he retorted. "People disappear around him. People the king dislikes. All too convenient." He tapped the side of his nose knowingly. "Some nobleman with a huge estate down south is gone, and notice this: the king now has the man's family manor! Vineyards and all. I heard the duke took care of that scoundrel Buckard, too. Do you realize that man still owes me a tenner?"

"The duke acted correctly in those matters." I wasn't going to mention my part in Lord Buckard or Count Westergaard's fate; the duke had broad enough shoulders to carry the blame, especially as he wasn't here to speak of my part in those events.

Jacques kept going. "His wife. One day she was happy, and the next gone. I think he had something to do with her death."

Yes, Jacques. Tristan Fontaine has told me he murdered his wife, Minette, and I am quickly finding reasons to convince myself that she probably deserved it.

I snapped, "Be careful, big brother, whom you slander. The duke might have *you* disappear. The way you talk about Minette Fontaine, you'd think you still bear a torch for her since her débutante days."

His brow went dark as thunder. "You don't know how I felt about her! Or what our relationship was. Where were you? Sequestered with your precious Morpheus Society, hanging out in graveyards and morgues. Would your father be happy to see you grubbing about with the gendarmes to solve the crimes of prostitutes and watch-thieves?"

Luckily for him, the cab rolled up to a stop, and I quickly disembarked with the experience of a city girl. To the driver, I handed up another bill. "Take my *friend* to the barracks, and quickly."

Seeing the number on the bill, he cracked the whip, and Jacques was slammed onto the backrest. Turning to look back at me, he gave me a terse military salute as the carriage sped away.

Chapter Nine

Standing on the steps to my mentor's old home, my hand on the railing, I flashed back to my first appearance here, when I was seventeen and my father had been dead less than two weeks.

It was here that Sergeant, now Inspector, Barbier had brought me, hoping spiritualism would provide fresh evidence to a case that had gone cold. I moved in with Madame Granger a month later as her student.

It was past midnight, but there was a light burning in the bottom window where the parlor was located. The door knocker was a woman's hand shaped in brass. I raised it and gently tapped, the noise echoing loudly in my imagination.

The door opened, and suddenly there stood Mysir Cédric Durant.

"Is Madame available?"

Madame's servant said nothing, but drew back from the door. I entered the narrow foyer smelling of beeswax, shadows, and ghosts.

Durant was an aloof, self-contained, inscrutable person. In the year I had lived with Madame Granger before moving into the

Society's dormitory for further training, I had learned little about him, only that he was a former sailor, and that from all the clever knots he could tie.

Madame Granger's parlor was called the garden room because of all the hand-colored lithographs of flowers she had on the wall. It was a room stuffed with her memories: daguerreotypes on the mantle and the piano, stacks of yellowing books and music sheets, and in a glass curio cabinet a stuffed parrot, one eye long lost. All had been there when I'd lived here, and would probably not be removed until she herself was taken out by the undertaker.

Durant closed the room's door, leaving without a word. The grate had a low fire in it. After stirring it up, I dropped another two coals on top from the scuttle using the brass tongs.

It was no more than ten minutes later that Madame Leona Granger entered the room. Like myself, she was a petite woman, with large faded blue eyes and masses of white hair piled on top like a cloud. Madame wore a loose robe dress tied at the waist that was appropriate for receiving guests at home.

I was right in remembering that she stayed up long into the night to talk with her ghostly acquaintances. She would sleep most of the day away, and rise a few hours after the luncheon hour. It made for a strange schedule, and it had taken me years to break myself from the habit after I'd left.

I went to her immediately to kiss both of her cheeks, smelling the old-fashioned floral scent of her perfume. The scent brought back memories of a foster-mother to a young girl shattered by her father's murder.

"Elinor, what a delight it is to see you."

Now in her seventies, she was the best medium the Morpheus Society had produced in the last forty years. Her palsy, which had been barely a tremor when I'd met her, was so severe now that it shook the handle of her waxwood cane. Struck suddenly by her frailty, I helped her to the most comfortable chair, positioning a pillow behind her back. She pulled her pink wooly capelet over her bony shoulders.

"You look so nice, Elinor. Have you made changes to your hair?"

"Thank you, Leona. No, it's the same. How have you been?"

"I'm seeing another doctor. Always another doctor, with some new syrup for me to take, but it will all result in nothing. But I let them think they can do something, so not as to damage the confidence of these young doctors."

The coals had caught, and the room was feeling a bit warmer. Finding a chair next to her, I sat down, preparing to be patient. There was no way to rush a conversation with her, and never had been, for she lived with her mind half listening to spirits.

Leona took her time about things, and over the years had developed a ritual of how she conducted our conversations. First we would talk of her health, for she was always consumed with the idea of the latest medical drug. Next it would be my father's murder, and finally she would push the idea that it was time for me to marry.

"Is there anything new about your father's murder? How is your investigation going?"

"I still have no answers or firm leads, but something odd did happen." I told her about how Marcus had found my father's watch, and how I'd used psychometry in an attempt to learn something from it.

"I personally have never found psychometry very reliable," she said, rather disdainfully. It was a method she was not good at, so she had no use for it. Given her contempt for it, I did not think she would believe me, so I did not share the knowledge that it had given me: that my father's killing had not been random, but done by someone he knew and trusted.

"It left a mark on me where it touched the skin." Unbuttoning my blouse's neckline, I showed her the area right below my left collarbone, where a crescent burn scar remained from where the watch had made contact with my skin.

Her cool fingers reached out, though she did not touch it. "A surreal mark made from a dream. Unusual."

"You see it? Thank goodness. A good friend of mine, a doctor, could not, and neither could my maid, Anne-Marie."

"So it is selective in showing itself? How interesting." Her eyes, faded with age, were still bright with intelligence.

"But what does it mean? I don't understand!" *And why could Archambeau see it?*

"I would not put too much thought into it, Elinor. Things often only seem mysterious. My guess? The watch was a locus, and it released energy when it came back to you. Like a piece of psychic coal, it sparked and marked you. It was simply a transfer of energy. I suspect your doctor and servant are simply ghost-blind, too grounded in the logical, real world to see the ethereal."

Having gained no insight, I buttoned my blouse back up, frustrated.

Madame Granger patted my cheek. "Goodness, child, don't take things so seriously."

Her words made me feel mulish. This was one of the reasons I had reduced my visits to my old mentor. As I'd gained experience, wanting to reach further, understand more that wasn't being taught, she had wanted to remain the teacher, the one with all the answers. It never went well for me to question any of her authoritative statements.

Of course, she saw my mood. I could hide little from her.

"Dear child, you cannot keep dwelling on the death of your father! We tried our best at the time, but he has moved on to the Afterlife."

"I will bring his killer to justice. You shall see."

She tutted. "Criminals like that lead such a life that he's probably already been put in a grave by some other thief."

"Dead or alive, I will find out who it is," I replied stubbornly. It was an old argument, and one that I had been having with her since her séance so long ago had failed to summon my father.

Seeing my stubbornness, Madame sighed and changed the subject. "How is that young girl working out for you as an apprentice? What was her name again?"

"Twyla Andricksson. She has a lot to learn."

Leona chuckled. "All of these young apprentices are nothing but a storm in a teacup. Everything blown out of proportion. Emotions everywhere— their minds are as hard to keep contained as a basketful of new kittens. How I remember the trouble you were! Turning up on my doorstep with a guardia, demanding that I find your father's killer, and when I did not have answers, did I receive any thanks for my effort? No, only curses that a sailor might know!"

Leona became lost in the past, a place that was far more real to her than today was. Perhaps I was doing her a disservice, but it made me think it was her way to remind me that I would forever be the apprentice, she the teacher.

"You weren't at all well-suited to being a medium. Do you remember? Too grounded in the real world, not the dreamy type at all. In my experience, it's the forgetful ones, the daydreamers who do best."

"Twyla Andricksson assures me that you told her she was a natural."

"Twyla? Oh yes, that new apprentice of yours. Well, spirits are attracted to her. Even when she was asleep they would show up, rapping and knocking, trying to get her attention. Turbulent energy, I imagine. She spilled the milk so many times that they removed her from the kitchen work roster at the dormitory."

That did make me smile, remembering the many clumsy accidents of my apprentice. Such as mistakenly using sugar instead of salt as a protection, which meant everyone had nightmares during an overnight stay in a haunted house. Or when she had demanded money from who she thought was a client when in fact they were a ghost.

"You like things so neat and contained, everything in their box, labeled and tidy. Twyla is the most untidy thing I've ever come across. Always asking why. Why did we wave the smoke clockwise and not counter-clockwise before a Ghost Talk? Why do some ghosts forget who they are and others don't? Oh, that one was stuffed with questions at the lectures."

"Asking questions can lead to new answers," I said, finding myself defending the girl.

Leona ignored me, following the path of her own tangled thoughts. "Nothing like you at all. Practical and grounded in the real world, you were. My house accounts were balanced for the first time. You even convinced the butcher to give us better cuts of meat at the same prices, something Durant can never achieve."

There was nothing I could do to sidetrack her, so I joined in with the remembrances. "You kept sending me to the attic for meditations. I couldn't think why, until I finally summoned that little girl spirit who died a hundred years ago."

She nodded her head in a bobbing motion that trembled with her palsy. "Yes, that's right. And the spirit couldn't speak. Lost her mind, long ago, and could only walk the halls as a repeater. Not much of a ghost, but you were so proud of making her materialize. Do you remember?"

"I do. I do remember." The blueness of her veins was clear under her pale skin dotted with liver spots. I picked her hands up and cradled them gently in my own, my anger forgotten. Tracing a random pattern in her palm with my forefinger, I mused, "I did wonder why Parnell sent Twyla to me. Do you know?"

"I'm sure he did it to upset you, Elinor. He's always looking for a way to score against you, and that girl needs so much patience that he probably thought she'd make you wild."

"Well, she has been a bit of a challenge." Coming finally to what I wanted to discuss, I asked nonchalantly, "Speaking of which, Twyla said Parnell was doing some sort of new research? Is it to do with these secretive parties he does with a girl medium?"

Her hands in mine did not move, showing she was not alarmed by my question. She only gave a sigh. "Oh, those things. So silly and dramatic. That's Lafayette's new idea of how the living can move safely into the Beyond. You gave him the idea."

"Me? I certainly did not!"

Leona tilted her head, peering at me through her white bangs, her messy bun of thick hair at the back of her head falling apart like stray cloud wisps. "Oh my, you certainly did. When you sent that paper on that ghost dragon to the committee, you threw a fox among the hens! A paper outlining how you, a living woman, created a reality in the Beyond, a place we believed only reserved for the dead. You didn't think he was going to ignore that? Of course he was going to try and duplicate what you did."

My stomach lurched, and I let go of her hands. Standing up, I went over and aggressively stirred the coals with the poker, sending sparks up the chimney. How could I be blamed for any of this?

"We already have too many at the sanatorium because of mediums losing their minds in the Beyond. How could he do this?" I turned to watch her answer, her face cast with the glow from the fireplace, while mine remained shadowed.

"As you should know, desperate people wanting answers will agree to anything," she retorted. "He's found some gullible girls who think what happens to others will never happen to them. Of course, he shows them the ones who failed. The inmates mindlessly pacing their cells, pounding the walls until their hands bleed, screaming themselves hoarse with nonsense. But does it stop them from wanting to try? Did it stop you? No."

"Did you not try to stop Parnell?" I asked sadly.

She retorted peevishly, "I have no more authority. I've stepped down from the committee chair."

"And they let you?" I was surprised. This was a development I knew nothing of. Certainly I've been out of the loop!

"I was forced out. No one wants to listen to us senior mediums anymore, not even you! Jarrod passed away peacefully in his sleep, and Dorothea wanted to spend more time with her grandchildren. Parnell and his people are in charge of everything now."

For her the topic was evidently closed, but I pressed anyway. "Have you heard mention of the name Ebbe Losendahl?"

"I don't recall it." She poked my dress skirt with her cane's point. "Elinor, why aren't you married? You'd make an excellent wife. And it's so much safer than chasing criminals. Don't you want to start a family of your own?"

CHAPTER TEN

After returning to the Crown, I did not sleep. I had too
much on my mind, and dawn was only a few hours away
anyway, so there seemed little point to it. Bathing and
dressing in fresh clothes, I put my hair up myself in a simple
chignon. Before leaving, I wrote a note for Anne-Marie, who
should be arriving sometime in the next hour.

I made my way to the Crown's dining hall and ordered coffee
and a pastry. It was not long afterward that the Duke de Archambeau entered the hotel lobby. Over the rim of my cup, I evaluated
him: tall, but not too tall; attractive, but not cloyingly handsome
like Lord Buckard. Yet there was something in how he walked, the
turn of his head, and the alert intelligence in his eye, which held
my attention.

After Archambeau spoke to one of the front desk clerks, he
made his way through the wide arch that marked the boundary
between the hotel lobby and its restaurant. Seeing me, he started
making his way through the deserted tables.

"Madame," he greeted me.

We were back to being formal, then. This back-and-forth with
how he addressed me kept me off balance. Was he doing this delib-

erately, this guessing game of what our friendship was? Two could play at this game.

"Your Grace. Have a seat. I'm almost finished. Do you wish for anything?"

"No, I breakfasted before leaving Hartwood," he replied, mentioning the name of his town home. Pierre, the head waiter, had started towards us at the duke's arrival, but at the shake of my head, he turned to greet two women who were seated at another table.

Archambeau leaned back in his chair, hands plaited together over his flat stomach. There was a moment's frigid silence before he said abruptly, "I returned last night to leave a note for you that I would have the inspector meet us here this morning, but the staff at the front desk said you were not in."

"No. After you left, I went to visit my old mentor, Leona Granger. Your words last night about the Society made me want to question her."

"Ah. I thought you decided to leave with your soldier friend."

"Jacques? No. Well, he wanted me to go out with him, but I sent him home. He should have left by now with his general. His unit is starting a tour of the outer provinces, and he will be gone all summer."

Archambeau turned over a cup at the table and, reaching over for the pot, poured himself coffee. He didn't sweeten it, taking it black. "Did your mentor have anything useful to impart?"

I worked at not sounding hurt.

"The leadership at the Society has changed. The old guard has stepped down and my nemesis, Parnell Lafayette, is now in charge. Because he knows that I went into the Beyond as a living person, I'm told he has been conducting research trying to duplicate the same. To make the living exist in the Beyond."

"Isn't that rather the opposite of what the parties do? Bringing ghosts here as if they are alive?"

I wiped my mouth, taking time to reply, carefully considering my words. "I think he's trying to reverse engineer the effect. It's that phrase Solberg used: *the living made dead*. I think that means there is an exchange. The living medium takes herself into the Beyond to exist in a half-dead state, and the dead come here to live."

"Unsettling." His voice was rough, and it made me examine him more closely. While his outfit of midnight blue was immaculate in styling and pristine in tailoring, his face bore signs of a restless night, with shadows under his eyes and a lock of ruffled hair that refused to stay with the others. Someone had not slept either.

"During a séance, a medium brings a ghost to them through a summoning— she or he calls out to a certain soul for a response, or we open a channel for whoever comes. That drugged drink seems to put the Chosen One completely under, which puts them at risk of being possessed, or not being able to end the medium connection when needed. You would be utterly helpless to whatever arrived from the Beyond."

"That does not sound good for the health of the Chosen One." Archambeau's fingers stroked the long handle of the silver coffee pot, his gaze contemplative as he stared unseeing at his reflection on its gleaming surface. "If Ebbe Losendahl is being used in such a manner, how long could she survive?"

"Again, it is only a theory."

"And theoretically?" He had little patience today, it seemed.

"It would weaken her, surely. How much I cannot say. Another cause of concern would be her lack of training. It could make her susceptible to unpleasantness."

"Do you know what it makes me think of?" said Archambeau.

"What?"

"In Zulskaya, when a mountain cat develops a taste for sheep, the shepherds have a way to catch it. They stake out a young lamb or baby goat to bring the creature close in order to kill the cat." He grimaced before adding, "Do you think these girls, the Chosen Ones, survive? Because it is in my thoughts that they do not."

I pushed my plate away and, feeling cold, put my gloves back on. "That is what I also fear."

"An early start to your day, Elinor," said Inspector Barbier. I immediately invited him to sit with us. Taking a seat, he said to Archambeau, "It's all arranged like you wanted, Your Grace."

"What's been arranged?" I asked.

Archambeau informed me. "We are going to Lafayette's lair, a set of consulting rooms in Bonecutter's Alley."

It wasn't exactly an alley where butchers and barbers plied their trade anymore, but the name had stuck. Now, it was the quarter of Alenbonné where doctors who cured both physical and mental ailments saw patients in comfortable offices. It was a very elite address, despite the name.

The inspector told us, "Dupont's been watching our man since last night and has sent word that Lafayette has arrived on the premises."

I stood up. "Shall we go then, gentlesyrs?"

~

Bonecutter's Alley was located at the opposite end of the city from the university, as if to disavow association with where the doctors actually learned how to cut and stitch. Here there were no rough tradesmen's delivery vans or street vendors hawking fruit and veg in their push carts. It was quiet, with mature trees starting to leaf, and nice broad sidewalks for a pleasant stroll.

When a carriage drove by, its horse leaving a fresh pile, a small boy with a broom and pan rushed out from some yard and cleaned it up. He disappeared, along with his full pan, back down a narrow alley between two buildings. It was all very tidy and very controlled.

We found a discreet sign with Parnell's name on the black iron gate outside a gray brick four-story. Parnell Lafayette's consulting rooms were located at the end of the lane and were not in the prime area of the block.

After a discreet tap at the black door, a housemaid in white cap and apron answered, only to be pushed back by the invasion of the inspector, the duke, and myself. The inspector demanded briskly, "Where can we find your employer?"

Intimidated into silence, she pointed to a closed door, which the duke promptly entered. We found Parnell Lafayette sitting at his desk, reading the morning paper. He looked up, his gaze traveling from Barbier (scornful dismissal), to Archambeau (mild curiosity) and finally to me (irritation).

Parnell's face was one of an ascetic: pale as old wax, with the skin tight over the bones as if he'd fasted for a week. His light blond hair was bleached straw over a domed head and while he was tall, it was a hunched form, as if his body was far older than his actual years. It had been eight years since I had seen him, and his unwell appearance shocked me, for he was only a few years older than I.

However, his voice was strong and deep. "Whom do I have the pleasure of meeting?"

Archambeau pulled out his full provincial title. "As you know, I am Mysir de Duke de Chambaux. This is Inspector Marcellus Barbier of the gendarmes, and my colleague, Madame Elinor Chalamet, with whom you have an acquaintance."

Inspector Barbier said firmly, "We would like your help with our inquiry into a delicate matter."

"Certainly." Parnell went past us to shut the door. He even moved like an old man, as if his joints hurt. Gesturing to the chairs in his room, he retook his former position behind the desk as we arranged ourselves. Archambeau drew a chair out for me, and after I sat, so did the inspector and the duke.

"How can I help you, gentlesyrs?"

I was surprised when Archambeau let the inspector ask the questions. In my experience, the duke was the one who preferred to be in command, but here he seemed to be playing a role. He flicked specks off the hat resting on his knee, and looked blandly around the room as if disinterested in the discussion.

Barbier said, "We've been informed that you are now the head of the Morpheus Society."

"Oh, I wouldn't say that. We are managed by a board of directors, of which I am one of several. I'm sure Madame Chalamet has told you how democratic we are. We take people from all walks of life, and all levels of education."

His stare I met calmly, perhaps even with a touch of amusement. I wasn't intimidated or insulted by his insinuations; I knew my worth.

Before either of us could see who would be the first to break their stare, something rubbed against my skirt, distracting me. At my feet was a black-striped tabby cat which, as cats do, jumped into my lap unasked. Instinctively, I started stroking my new friend with my gloved hand while it kneaded my jacket.

The inspector pressed. "So, you are one of the men who would be at the top. Someone who would know if the organization was holding parties of a questionable nature?"

If we were expecting him to look shocked or to confess, we were all sadly disappointed.

"Parties? We do hold ones for fundraising, and have social mixers where members can meet each other."

I spoke up for the first time. "You forgot our annual meeting, Mysir Lafayette. I hear you will be presenting some unique research based upon my own findings of the Beyond that I submitted to the Society."

His eyelids gave a quick trembling flutter, a tell I knew of old: he was suppressing strong emotions. Given the right match, he could catch fire. "Unlike your allegations, mine will be based upon solid research and be backed with actual facts."

Before I could make another attempt to flame up his temper, Barbier went on. "These parties I'm asking about are specialized things. A woman conducts what seems to be a very powerful séance, where party-goers interact with the dead in ways that would be frowned upon by the courts."

Lafayette laughed, but it sounded false to me. He shook his head sadly, as if exasperated by the very idea the inspector had put forth. "Oh, Inspector, these rumors! I've heard it all. There are always people who will make sensational statements and use ghosts as a gimmick to fool the gullible. Why, last year there was that woman, Madame Nyght, with her fake ectoplasm and table-turnings, who fleeced merchants and aristos alike. We at the Society take a very dim view of that. We are about method and logic, which can be reproduced under a strict scientific method."

"I complained several times about Madame Nyght to the Society, to no avail," I reminded him.

His eyelids did a another quick flutter as he said tersely, "The matter was resolved."

"By the law!"

He grimaced as if tasting something sour. I am sure he would have liked to throw the crystal paperweight on his desk at my head.

Barbier said, "That may be true, mysir; however, that doesn't mean that all of your members are as scrupulous as you are. I have a Royal Warrant to obtain the list of members of your organization, and for the names of those who have attended your lecture series at the Hall of Science."

At first I didn't think Parnell would comply, but after a moment he reluctantly drew out from a lower desk drawer two ledgers and set them on the desk. "May I ask why you need this information?"

Barbier sent a sidelong glance at Archambeau as if expecting him to say something, but when he did not, told Parnell, "We are looking for a missing woman. Lady Ebbe Losendahl. Have you heard of her? Seen her?"

At each question, Parnell shook his head. "No. Why would I have?"

I spoke up again. "We have reason to believe she reached out to someone in the Morpheus Society, seeking a mentor."

"I shall ask among the members, but no, I personally have not heard of her," said Parnell. In a bored manner, he handed over the books and, indicating the door with his outstretched hand, said, "Now, I have answered your questions, so perhaps I could be left to prepare for my day filled with clients?"

Kitty butted its head under my chin for attention. I cradled it against my shoulder and took a deep breath of its fur before setting it down on the floor.

Last to exit, I felt Parnell's stare in the middle of my shoulder blades. Thankfully, it wasn't a heavy paperweight— or a knife.

CHAPTER ELEVEN

Standing on the stoop, the men talked while I considered what I had learned.

"I'll take this list to the station and start reviewing it," Barbier said.

Archambeau took the book from the guardia and flipped through pages of names as he walked slowly down the three steps to the sidewalk. "That shall take some time."

"Is there anything else we can do?" asked the inspector, in a tone that didn't expect much of an answer.

The duke grimaced. "We are hitting dead ends. Hopefully, something will stand out on the list."

The quick-cab that the inspector had hailed stopped at the curb and he got in. The duke handed him back the ledgers as Barbier asked, "Are you coming down to the station?"

"You go on, inspector, we shall meet up later," said the duke, taking my arm to prevent me from leaving, if I had thought to do so. The cab pulled away down the tree-lined boulevard. Archambeau steered me in the opposite direction, and we started down the promenade.

"Tell me your thoughts about Parnell, Chalamet, and I will share mine."

I held up my free hand and said, "Smell this."

He gave me a quizzical look, but did as I asked. "Leather? And something else? Like a child's candy stick."

"It's a licorice smell, don't you think? With a hint of something a little fishy? I was rubbing his cat, and this is what scented my glove. I think it's from the solution used to drug the women, and if I'm right, that means Parnell *is* involved!"

Archambeau touched his hat in greeting to someone who passed us before asking me, "How can you be so sure?"

"Identifying concoctions by smell and taste is one of the skills the Morpheus Society trains us to practice. This one combines two powerful narcotics— the poppy and an oil from a fish sac. Both encourage euphoria, perhaps even hallucinations, before the recipient goes into a deep sleep. If used in too high a dose, you might not wake up."

"You've used these?" He stopped walking in order to face me, his expression shocked.

I was quick to reassure him. "No! The Society actually warns against them, because they are dangerous and addictive. Trust me, I have no interest in being lost in dreams or the Beyond! However, we are trained to know what they can do and how to identify them."

Reassured by my answer, he resumed our stroll. "Why would a cat's fur smell like that? If it is so dangerous, surely anything like you've described would kill a cat?"

"I imagine anything related to fish would be attractive to cats, don't you think? I'm thinking the cat was either in the room at some time when it was being created, or got into the supplies. It must have had very little contact in order to survive. We should visit Charlotte today and ask her about these drugs, as my knowledge is very limited. Perhaps she would have a list of herbalists or chemists that carry it? She should be free from classes in about another hour."

"That would give us another line of inquiry and possibly hard evidence against him. We will need that if we want to bring Lafayette to justice."

I nodded in agreement. "Now you. What were you looking at while the inspector was asking all those questions?"

"First, Parnell knew we were coming."

"What?!" This time it was I who stopped walking out of surprise.

"Yes. The paper he was supposedly reading when we arrived? You couldn't see it, as he put it away when you came in behind us, but it was a week old. An article about a road sewer repair in one of the outlying districts. Not exactly a compelling read. The man was waiting for us, that I am sure."

Looking both ways at the corner, and finding the street deserted except for one old lady in her carriage being driven at a sedate pace, we crossed to the canal side. I found the lifelessness of the district depressing. Give me the bustle of the hotel district, or even the shabby bravado of the university area, over this catatonic neighborhood any day.

"But who would have told him?" I asked Archambeau.

"Obviously someone at the gendarmes. It's why I did not want to join the inspector. What do you know of Barbier?"

"It's not him," I said stoutly. "His lameness is from a fall when he was pushed out of a second-story window by a man he was chasing for murder. That experience gave him a rabid devotion to fighting criminals. Marcellus would never compromise an investigation by leaking information, even innocently."

"Dupont?"

"I don't know him well," I admitted. "Marcellus took him on about two years ago as a transfer from another station. The man's a blank wall."

"Perhaps he feigns stupidity?"

"You think him secretly cunning? Have you tried having a conversation with him? I suppose I could see him being questioned by a smarter person and letting the cat out of the bag without meaning to."

"Hm. It's something to consider."

We paused at the top of the humpback bridge and, as I always did, I stared over the railing down into the canal, watching the swirling water. Alenbonné was a town of water, and some said between that and the limestone, which seemed to act as a conduit for spiritual energy, it made the place a home to ghosts.

"Why didn't you ask Parnell any questions?"

"In interrogation it is helpful to have one ask and the other watch. It can reveal certain things about the suspect's character when their words do not."

"And what did his face reveal?"

Archambeau drummed his fingers against the steel railing, drawing the quacking ire of a couple of ducks who were swimming under us. "He truly dislikes you, Elinor."

My mood lifted at the use of my first name. He didn't use it often, and sometimes I wondered if he realized that he had, for usually he would return to a more formal address or simply address me as Chalamet as one would a male colleague.

"That doesn't surprise me at all. We disliked each other intensely when we were all in training."

"I noticed his books are all titles about diseases. Mostly terminal ones."

"His parents died from long, lingering illnesses: his father from a brain tumor and his mother of a breast infection. It's probably why he was drawn to the Society in the first place, like many of us are. I remember Parnell was always anxious about his health. It was rather a joke among us at the time."

"I did think the texts on embalming were a bit morbid."

Perhaps they were to someone who didn't speak with ghosts. I hoped he wasn't going to judge my collection anytime soon. "It's been some time since we have met, and what struck me is how ill the man looks. If we can get Charlotte to look at him, we should, for the man does not look well."

"I'd like to go with you to visit Dr. LaRue."

"You're welcome to."

"But first, I think? Something to eat?"

"Have I ever said no to that?"

He took my arm, and we crossed another street, and since the day was pleasant for spring, we selected an outdoor table at a café. A tray of mid-morning appetizers arrived, along with a bottle of Chambaux wine. Since the duke was paying, I was quite happy with the extravagance.

"I don't see Parnell as a killer. As an enticer of young girls who could give him access to the Beyond, yes," I said, popping an olive into my mouth.

"I agree. Mys Wahl was killed by a professional, or at the least someone practiced in the act. I doubt Parnell has the strength to hold a healthy woman still long enough to kill her."

"Why do you say that?" While I had worked with the gendarmes for some time, my actual experience was in talking with ghosts, not examining bodies.

"The cut was clean. No hesitation. Most first-time killers don't know how forcefully they need to use the knife, so usually the skin will show other cuts that are not as deep or effective."

"Oh." I didn't want to think about that while spreading my jam on a scone. That poor girl. "I had a note from Charlotte left at the desk late last night telling me that Mys Wahl was indeed pregnant."

"It may be best for Dr. LaRue to hold that information back from the girl's parents when the body is returned home. They won't want to know their daughter died as a sullied blossom, I'm sure."

"How like a man! She was a woman who was in love."

"That won't stop society from condemning her."

"From the man whose peers think it is fine for a married woman to take lovers! What hypocrisy!"

"And that is where you don't understand the subtleties of my class, Elinor. Mys Wahl was not married. If Mys Wahl had been wed, the child would be assumed to be her husband's. If society thought it not, while there might be gossip, the child would still be accepted. It's why women are encouraged to seek lovers from their own level or higher. If a man has a cuckoo in his nest, and he is but a lord, and the sire of the babe an earl, it reflects well upon everyone."

I shuddered. "Barbaric and disgusting."

"It seems immensely practical to me."

"Truly? Would you be fine with a wife who bore another man's child?"

His shrug told me a lot about his marriage.

Pouring out a second glass for us both, I said, "Of course, you married without love, so perhaps you wouldn't be jealous of your wife straying."

He laughed again without mirth. "Marrying once was enough for me."

"But you don't have an heir," I pointed out.

"After Minette died, I dug up a second cousin, and he's at Chambaux now learning how to manage the estate. Mother isn't happy about that, but I've settled an annuity upon her and told her I would not discuss it any further."

I hid behind my glass, digesting what he had said. Distracted, I barely heard him return to the subject of our victim.

"Do you believe Mys Wahl's parents would be happy to hear their daughter was bearing a bastard from an incompetent, third-rate street artist?"

"That's cold-blooded."

He pressed his point. "Are you saying that I'm wrong?"

Sadly, I did not think he was. Society, both high and low, took a dim view of a woman bearing a child outside of wedlock. Probably in the duke's world, such a woman would quietly have the baby at some resort and it would later be adopted by some cousin. That would not have been the future of Mys Wahl's child.

"Let us go over what we know at this point," said Archambeau. "Lady Losendahl is in a depressed state of mind, still morose over the death of her friend. Upon meeting the duplicitous Mysir Solberg, she learns of the Society."

I added to his observation. "Obviously she wants to contact her dead friend, so prepares a trip under false pretenses to meet someone who can help her. She does not think she will be coming back from what she plans on doing, as evidenced by the giving away of her possessions."

Archambeau countered, "Although this doesn't seem to be known by her maid, Mys Wahl, who in a panic contacts her lover when her mistress doesn't return. Later, she also leaves and unfortunately meets her death."

"Probably she got a note. The hotel didn't seem aware of any written or oral message, so hand-delivered most likely? That could be an avenue to research. I'm sure the estimable Madame Travers would know."

He shook his head in admiration. "What a woman. She needs to be on the stage or working at a newspaper, not managing chambermaids."

"Why was Mys Wahl, and not Lady Losendahl, found dead in an alley? Where is she?"

"I'd say that Lafayette has further need of her. These damnable parties."

Unnoticed by Archambeau, a woman at the next table glared at us, shocked at his curse word. I hid my smile behind my napkin.

Chapter Twelve

With morning classes done, we found Charlotte in her office. Her door was open and when she saw the two of us, she waved us to enter with one hand while writing on a piece of paper with the other.

"Your Grace, Elinor. I'm wrapping this up. Take a seat."

Her massive desk, a thing she referred to as The Beast, took up half the room. I've often wondered how it had been placed there, for its width was wider than her narrow door. She joked that the room had probably been built up around it, and since the university offices for the teaching staff were cut out in odd sizes, she might have been right.

It was a tight squeeze, and Archambeau stopped a stack of professional journals from toppling over just in time as we made our way to the two black leather and walnut low-backed chairs.

Each wall had a floor-to-ceiling bookcase that Charlotte had put together herself, so they were cut with odd sizes to fit her personal collection. Despite her handiwork, there wasn't enough room on the shelves for everything, so books were double-stacked and some with volumes set behind the other. Or they were wedged in so tightly that the books bulged outward, groaning.

There was a dirty window at the top of the exterior wall. In the rays that struggled through, dust motes danced all the way down to Charlotte's desk. There was little surface to spare between stacks of student papers, a thick medical reference book on human anatomy, a stray stethoscope, an equal-armed, analytical balance scale with a row of lead weights, and for some reason, an unopened jar of jam.

There was a knock at the open door. A young man with a very wispy mustache, that he was probably exceedingly proud of, put his head around the jamb. Seeing us, he stopped mid-sentence. Charlotte waggled her pencil at him. "What? Out with it, Nikolas. These two won't bite."

Regaining control of himself, the young man said, "Dr. Rutherford wanted to know if you were staying in for lunch. Did you want something brought back?"

Charlotte gave a quick look at the clock on her desk and replied, "Why didn't you come by sooner? Never mind. Yes, bring me back a bottle of ginger beer, and a meat pastry. Don't buy it at that place you lot go to. You may enjoy mystery meat, but I do not. Go down to the corner and get it from Gertrude's." She dug in her trouser pocket and brought out a wad of bills and some change. "Do you two need anything?"

"No, Charlotte. We are fine."

Nikolas ducked in and took the money from her, while Charlotte continued calling out her instructions. "And no pickle! I don't know why they keep wrapping it up with a damn pickle."

Nikolas didn't respond but scurried away down the hall, causing Charlotte to get up and shout down the hallway after him. "If you bring that back with a pickle, you'll need tongs to remove it from your throat!"

She returned, rubbing her hands briskly, and said to us in the benevolent manner of a favorite uncle giving the children a special treat during the holidays, "I'm sure you two want to discuss our latest dead body."

"Yes, we do," I said.

Behind her, from her shelves, Charlotte picked the top journal off a stack of six. From experience, I knew these books contained her case notes. She flipped past a couple of pages that had sketches of the body, refreshing herself with the details.

"Hannah Wahl, a young woman in her early twenties, maybe the upper teens."

"Baron Losendahl said she was nineteen," clarified Archambeau.

Charlotte made a note on her journal page before continuing. "I won't go into all the details we've already discussed. There are defensive wounds on her hands, small nicks and a few broken nails. But the majority of the bruising is across the upper chest. I guess the killer held her from behind like this."

She demonstrated by wrapping one arm around her own upper chest, just below her collarbone, but above her breast.

"He probably held her against him while he slit her throat." She made a slashing motion with her right hand, running her thumbnail over her neck.

"His Grace said it was one cut, which means our killer was probably experienced?"

"I'd agree with that assessment. Or if not a killer of humans, perhaps a butcher of animals? Or a doctor." At the last she gave an amused snort. "Wouldn't that be funny, if it was someone from this department? Can't imagine any of them having the energy, though."

"Anything on the type of knife that was used?" Archambeau asked.

"Probably a boning knife. Something you'd use for deer or hogs. A slightly curved, six- to eight-inch blade would work." Flipping to the back of her journal that had blank pages, she sketched it out while describing it to us. "See, like this. Can't say much about the handle, but probably at least four, if not five, inches long."

"Right or left-handed?" asked the duke.

"Right. The slash is left to right."

I told her, "I got your note this morning about Hannah."

"Yes, the poor girl was about fourteen weeks along. Do you want me to inform the family?"

I gave a heavy sigh before glancing over at my companion. Archambeau shrugged, leaving the decision in my hands.

"I think we need to tell Baron Losendahl and let him decide what to tell the family. After all, he actually knows them and we don't."

With sudden interest, Charlotte asked, "Will the family want the body? Or is it available to my students? Some are already asking."

This time the duke spoke up. His words were cool and unemotional. "I'm afraid your students will need to pick some other unfortunate. The baron wants her returned to his estate and will bear the cost of the train trip back in a mail express carriage."

Charlotte seemed to have no regret at his decision. "Alright. I'll get the paperwork and the packing done today. Though my advice is best not to leave the burial too long."

"I'll pass that along," he said.

She ripped out the page and handed the drawing to Archambeau, before closing the journal and returning it back on the stack. "There's not much more to say about poor Mys Wahl."

Looking down and removing a piece of lint from his trouser knee, Archambeau asked, "Was she violated?"

"Actually, no."

"That's some consolation, I suppose," I muttered.

"One thing from my experience: it does look like the fight took place before she had her throat slit," said Charlotte. "That might indicate two different men. One that used his fists and another with a knife. Or a man who beat her before killing her."

"Two men?" I mused.

Archambeau told her, "We spoke to Inspector Barbier, and he

said this is the first young lady you've had in the morgue for several months."

"Well, I'd have to check my records to be sure, but yes that seems about right." Swiveling again, she took down a massive tome from a shelf at eye level and dropped it on the desk with a thud. Its weight made the pencils jump. She flipped the cover open, revealing sheets with columns: the record of Alenbonné's dead that passed through her office. Her forefinger ran down the list.

"How far do you want me to go back?"

"Six months?"

"How young are we talking about? I've got a few dead babies, a nine-year-old and a twelve-year-old."

"No babies, but the twelve-year-old could be a possibility. What did she die of?" asked Archambeau.

"Father bashed her brains in."

"No. That isn't what we're looking for."

"I have an eighteen-year-old, unidentified female, that was hit by a train? What about that one?"

"A possibility."

"I'll write down a description for you."

While Charlotte wrote down the particulars, I put forth my questions about the use of the poppy and the fish sac from the Scarlet Moon-Eye.

"Yes, well, the poppy was used for anesthesia, but we already have far more modern methods now."

"But how does—?"

"What Madame Chalamet is trying to ask is, how do you use poppy and what effects does it give? Not being a drug user, she's unfamiliar with its properties."

"Oh, I see. Yes. Hm. Well, it's mostly used for recreational purposes. It's brought in from Perino. Add it to hemlock and you have a nice cocktail for a painless death. I've seen a few suicides use that method. It's legal through your physician. You can take it as a tincture for insomnia or pain. I think I saw a paper recently about it."

She got up and started searching through the pile of journals that we had almost toppled. Not immediately finding what she wanted, she returned to her desk.

"I'll search for it later. However, I do remember the article saying it was very habit-forming. It's interesting, though, how some will develop a craving for it, yet others don't."

"Can you drink it?" I asked.

"Drink it, eat it, smoke it. Whatever takes your fancy."

"What about this fish sac thing Madame Chalamet mentioned?"

"Oh, the Scarlet Moon-Eye? That's more exotic." Again, Charlotte stood and, using a stepstool, reached high above my head to bring down another book. She started at the back, looking at a reference page before turning to the middle of the volume. She showed us a picture of a very round fish with bulging eyes and small fins. "Here's our fish friend."

"I've never seen anything like that before," said the duke. "How hard is it to find one of those?"

"Hm, not too hard. They are a bit of a pest on the fringe of our fishing waters down south. They often come up in nets. Fishermen will toss them back because Moon-Eyes don't taste good and their poison sac makes trouble if it bursts and mixes with the other fish. The toxin from the sac is sometimes harvested for ecstatic rituals. The kind where people dance naked around a bonfire under the moon, as they imagine their brains being sucked out by giant ants. According to student gossip."

"So it only provides hallucinations?" I asked.

Charlotte scratched the side of her head with the eraser end of her pencil. "Well, truth be told, a lot of things can give some sort of excitement if you take it in small doses. And almost everything can kill you if you ingest enough, as our dear king proved."

I told her briefly about the parties we had been told about. Her eyebrows climbed.

"Drugged girls? Ghosts made flesh? I'd say the guests were drunk or high on something. That fish would do it. Certainly sounds bizarre enough."

Chapter Thirteen

After leaving Charlotte, the duke had an appointment to meet the baron and update him on our progress. For myself, I returned to my suite at the Crown, where I was enthusiastically greeted by my apprentice.

"How did it go with Mysir Lafayette? Did he confess? Did you arrest him? Did you find Lady Losendahl?"

"I'm afraid not." I unpinned my hat in front of the mirror and smoothed down my hair. Twyla's disappointed face showed in the reflection beside my own. "What did you discover? Anything?"

She flipped open a little notebook that I was amused to see was the same type Inspector Barbier used. She was taking her investigative work seriously.

"I went through the records of the morgue. That's what the news sheets call the basement, where they keep all the back copies of the paper. Isn't that a funny name? The personal ads were a gold mine. Although I kept getting distracted with those seeking lost loves and missing heirs."

"The missing heir advertisements are always some swindle game, Twyla. Never answer them."

"They are? But they sound so sincere. Listen to this one:

Mysirs Lockbridge and Timmons are looking for a young lady with brown hair and green eyes, left as an infant at the Maystay orphanage. You will have a locket with the initials RE. A reward is forthcoming to worthy individuals providing valuable information that resolves this inheritance issue."

I was in the middle of a laugh when I frowned. "Wait." Going to my room, I pulled out a soft pouch from my dresser drawer, where I had stored the locket received from Madame Chapelle. Returning to the parlor, I turned it around to show the back of the locket to Twyla.

"It says RE! Madame Chapelle's daughter must be the lost heir!" said the girl excitedly.

"As I told you, Twyla, these things are a confidence game. What I think is that someone wants to know where Madame Chapelle's daughter is. When did that announcement run?"

Twyla looked over her notes. "A week ago."

"So at least a month after the poor girl killed herself. Come, let's sit." We took adjoining seats on the sofa. "Have you ever tried any psychometry?"

"I'm not very good at it."

"Well, that's why I'm here. To teach you. Now, hold it in your hands. No, take off your gloves. Your flesh needs to touch it. We begin like any meditation— clear your mind first."

"I can't do it! I think too much."

"We'll try a different path, then. Keep your eyes open and look at the locket. Examine it very closely and tell me everything you see. Stay focused on it and nothing else."

"The chain is long, but of poor quality. It doesn't match the color of the locket. It looks to be a gray metal, something cheap."

"Yes, it's a machine-made cable chain, probably of some composite like nickel and zinc."

Encouraged by my words, Twyla continued examining it. "At one point, the chain was repaired. No, it was fixed at two points. The links are bent, as if someone used pliers and pinched too hard. And the chain's clasp doesn't match the metal. It looks newer."

"What does that tell us?"

"It wasn't original to the locket. Bought later? Fixed because she didn't have money to even replace a cheap chain?"

I nodded. "Go on. Think like a jeweler."

"The locket is gold colored, but not gold. From the nicks, it shows a gray metal underneath, so I'm guessing it's brass-plated. The RE on the back is well done, though. A bit fancy on the engraving for such a common piece, I would have thought, but the initials are worn like the rest of the locket, so it was probably done at the same time the locket was made."

She opened it, revealing nothing inside. I handed her my jeweler's loupe for her to examine it closer. "There's something stuck in the latch. A bit of dark brown or black hair, and in the recess, a tiny bit of paper."

"Ordinary paper, or that of a daguerreotype?"

"Oh! Let me see! I'm not sure?" She looked to me for an answer.

I felt the slick paper between my fingers and then sniffed it. It had a chemical smell to me. "A daguerreotype would be my guess. Unfortunately it is gone. We should ask her mother if she knew what it was. Or if she removed it herself."

"Why would she do that and not tell us?"

I smiled, shaking my head. "It could have been a photo she wanted to keep out of sentimentality— for example, an image of her daughter's father. Or Madame Chapelle didn't want us to see because it reflected poorly upon her daughter— like a lover. Now fold the locket into your hands, like this." I placed my own over hers. "Close your eyes." She did so, and I leaned forward, putting my forehead against hers. "Let me guide you."

It took a moment to focus on it, but soon the secrets of the locket started unfolding. Surely, something so long cherished would have a story to tell?

A dark-haired girl with green eyes gave the cold metal a kiss and pulled it over her head. Laying it on her bosom, she opened it, revealing a photo of an older man wearing mutton-chop whiskers and a full beard. A style popular with mature men, so my guess would be a father, coinciding with the story her mother had given of the locket being a gift from him. *The locket glowed with love and care.* Impressions faded away. I pulled my hands back; what information it could give us was done.

"That's psychometry? I've never felt that before." Twyla's eyes shone. "But how does that fit in with the lonely hearts advertisement?"

"That is something for you to figure out as your first case."

"Really?!"

Her obvious excitement made me feel guilty for being upset with her before. Truly, the girl just needed direction and patience, even if she could at times be annoying. "Yes. The locket didn't show us anything about her dying, so I suspect she wasn't wearing it when she passed. The classified seems strangely specific to me. Like they are looking for the locket, or maybe someone who owns the locket. Now, listen carefully, Twyla. I forbid you to answer that ad alone. You will work with Inspector Barbier on this, or I will end your apprenticeship."

She bobbed her head. "I will. I promise. But can't we do the same thing with the earring we found on Mys Wahl's body?"

"Yes, we can, and I certainly plan on doing so." I pulled it out of the felt storage bag where I had kept the locket. Twyla tapped her toes in gleeful excitement. "But before we do so, tell me if you discovered anything else."

"Two girls seem likely candidates: Lorraine Kaplan and Renee Bassett. There were multiple listings pleading for information and when I went by to visit with the families, they didn't seem likely to be runaway types. Both come from merchant families. Lorraine was actually engaged to be married to a man she loved. Renee was supposed to leave for a visit to country relatives and was looking forward to the trip."

"Did the two know each other?"

"Not as far as I could figure out. But they did both belong to the same circulating library. A small social club attached to a certain sweets and coffee shop. They could have met each other there."

"Very good work, Twyla. This sounds like a place we should visit."

"Right now?"

My hand on hers stopped the girl from impulsively leaping to her feet. "No, let's take a look at Ebbe's earring first."

"Oh, right."

I pulled back the folds of my lacy handkerchief and revealed again the large pearl with its diamond bow. It was a very pretty object; seeing it again made me think that Mys Wahl would only have worn such an object if she were meeting a man. Why wear anything so valuable during the day just to meet an ordinary friend? Maybe she would have done so to show it off. It was a shame that we really didn't know much about her personally, so could only guess at her motivations.

Again, I had Twyla hold it in her palms. "Keep them open this time." I laid my own open palms on top, sandwiching the earring between us. "Let us see if it can tell us anything important."

Using psychometry would yield different information than Ghost Talking a body. Objects weren't as reliable, as they retained fleeting impressions, and what those would be was unpredictable. For instance, the Chapelle locket had only shown us what I would expect: how it had been worn, its owner, and what emotional impressions had soaked into it over a lengthy period of time.

On the other hand, my father's watch had revealed the violence of his death. Why, I wasn't sure. Perhaps because he had been wearing it at the time, and the murderer had taken it with him? Would Ebbe's earring give us such important information?

Once the pearl and diamonds opened to us, images were revealed quickly. First of Ebbe, the original owner. It was odd to see her in motion. The serious, athletic girl from the daguerreotype was now smiling and moving. Elaborate dinner parties with the baron and a brown-haired woman matching him in age whom I assumed to be her mother.

But underneath these images was an unpleasant, disturbed hum. It was a vibration that I knew from experience had a connection to violent death. Not from accidents, but from murder.

Twyla tried to pull her hands away.

"No, not yet. Stay with me."

"But—"

"Stay with me," I commanded, wanting the information the earring could give us.

"But Elinor! He's back!"

The fright in her voice made me open my eyes. "Who's back?"

But she didn't have to answer, for I saw who she meant: the ghost Twyla had accidentally summoned in Madame Chapelle's parlor was here. Mysir Vonn, whose killing spree in the Hells had made him a legend. He was standing in front of us. If he had been a ghost, I could have handled him easily enough. But he was flesh, as solid as Twyla and myself.

"What an unpleasant surprise," I said, forcing myself to appear calm. Vonn's uncanny appearance was just more evidence that supernatural norms were being overturned.

He held up his hand, showing that he held a sharp-pointed knife, a match to the one Charlotte had drawn for us. The metal of the blade had a luster to it that drew the eye. "Our last time together was far too brief."

Twyla and I retreated, putting the couch between us and the madman. That wouldn't buy us much time. If I was to die, I wanted answers first. "You killed Hannah Wahl, didn't you?"

"The black-haired wench had it coming. Meeting lovers in

back alleys. *My* alley. She came to my favorite place as if waiting for me. A gift I couldn't say no to."

Questions flooded my brain, while fear kept me paralyzed. A ghost might cause injury or an accident, such as knocking out someone with a saucepan, but there was no documented case of them actually killing anyone. Yet. I didn't want to go down in history as the first. Oh, how I wished I had my man-stopper with me! But it was stowed in my wardrobe closet in my bedroom.

"Where did you come from? Why are you here?"

"The earring drew me. I have the match." Digging in his pocket, he brought out Ebbe's missing earring.

I told Twyla urgently, "You need to run to the kitchen. There's a fire ladder outside the window."

"No. I'm not leaving you here," she muttered, defiant.

"He's not shifting," I warned her. Since his appearance, I had been attempting to send him back to the Beyond. For some reason, all my efforts were failing.

At that moment the door to the suite opened and Anne-Marie entered, her arms full of clean towels she had probably collected from the Crown's laundress. Before she could react, Vonn lunged at her.

Grabbing a vase off the table, I threw it, screaming at him.

But it was Twyla who did the smartest thing. She grabbed my hand and transported us into the Beyond.

Chapter Fourteen

The world tilted as we shifted into the Beyond, a place meant only for the dead.

Instead of finding myself in the duke's conservatory, where I had battled the ghost-dragon, I was standing in a filthy narrow alley, the walls of the tenements towering so high that I couldn't see the sky.

While I was still disoriented, trying to make sense of what had just happened, Twyla pulled at my wrist, shouting, "Run!"

It was then that I saw Vonn, a few yards from where we stood. The spree killer was shaking his head, as confused as I was. Not waiting, Twyla and I started running.

"Did you bring us here? Or was it Vonn?"

"I brought us! But I think we're in Vonn's mind— where he resides in the Beyond." Twyla was speaking over her shoulder in panting breaths as we ran full tilt, our skirts hitched up. We dodged around trash barrels and jumped over brick rubble.

Twyla's guess seemed to be accurate, for we were running for our lives through a tenement alley typical of what was found in the Hells. There had been no time for me to shape reality, and I doubted that Twyla would have picked this type of scenery, so that left only our murderer.

The oddness of the Beyond always presented itself in little things, such as the lack of smell; there was no stench of sewage or garbage. No rats scurried away from our hurried approach. While we ran, our footsteps made no sound on the pavement below us. It was a shadow of reality, like dreams were.

I passed a window with shutters half askew on their hinges for the third time, and realized we were running through the same alley again and again. The area seemed to last about twenty feet before it repeated itself with the same garbage can, the same pile of broken bottles, and the broken shutters. The creation of the place was limited by the ghost's imagination, and Vonn only remembered his favorite alley enough to reproduce it, and even then, imperfectly.

I did not look back, but could hear Vonn's shouted expletives behind us.

"Return us to the Crown!" I shouted to Twyla.

"I can't without taking him! He's linked to us somehow."

While our surroundings might not behave like a real place, my body did, and it was tiring. The alley kept stretching onward, endless. No, I was wrong! There was a light ahead of us, like the dawn on the horizon. It made a bright void with no perceivable bottom. Thinking of how the ghost dragon had fallen into nothingness, I automatically slowed down, but a male shout behind me acted as a spur.

Grabbing Twyla by the arm, I ran into that brightness. A few moments later, an explosion happened behind us that sent us flying back to land on the ground. My ears ringing, I gazed around, befuddled. I did not feel the killer's spirit and realized that Vonn had not been able to follow us. Why, I did not know, but I was thankful for the reprieve.

Twyla asked with wonder, her voice echoing, "What is this? A palace?"

I could see why she thought so, for the place was extravagant in size. We stood in a large hall, museum-like, with an arched ceiling supported by pencil-thin columns in blood-red marble. The walls were plaster, a gray putty in color, and hanging on them were paintings all in gold ornamental frames. Strangely, when I tried to focus on the art to see what it was, it was like looking at something through a fogged window. Just blobs of color.

"Do you notice that when you look at the paintings, they go out of focus?"

"Yes!" Twyla went over to a wall in an attempt to see one of them close up, but as she approached, the wall moved away so she never reached her goal. She gave me a quizzical look.

"Don't ask me. I've never seen anything like it. Let's go through here." I pointed at one of the passageways between the columns.

We entered yet another room that mimicked the hall we had just left, with its arched roof and thin supporting columns. Here there were no paintings, but art of a different type. As we walked through it we discovered that between the columns were white marble statues of women, five in total. Each woman was mounted on a rectangular block plinth to raise her higher than normal human height, and one block was empty.

"That one is Renee Bassett!" cried Twyla, rushing over to one of the statues. Unlike the paintings, nothing moved, and she actually reached it. Hm. That meant, for some reason, the statues were more real than the paintings.

I came up behind her and looked up at the one she'd indicated. "How can you tell?"

"Her parents showed me a daguerreotype of her."

Renee must have been young, for she still had that baby roundness to her face, though her figure had blossomed into a woman's. Indeed, all the women were carved to appear as if dressed in thin drapery which hugged their body. If a man had been present, I would probably have blushed. Renee's lips were small and pouty;

her blank marble eyes were set wide on either side of a short, snub nose. The girl's hair was dressed in an elaborate coil of curls on top of her head, similar in style to all the other statues.

"Is Lorraine Kaplan here?"

"I didn't see a picture of her, so I don't know."

While we could not confirm it yet, I suspected she was here among us. I reached out a hand and lightly touched the robe of Renee Bassett.

As I made contact, a burning shock raced up my fingers to elbow, then shoulder. I snapped my hand back quickly. For a moment, it felt like the sightless eyes looked down at me. Whatever was behind that gaze was no longer human. I took a step back.

"I didn't know we had visitors," said a feminine voice.

The woman emerged from around a corner, and I gasped. It was Ebbe Losendahl! She was dressed in the same style as the statues: a clinging, winding sheet, her feet in sandals, and her curled hair piled high. As I had guessed from her photo, she was tall, making the woman next to her appear even shorter. Her companion was dressed in the same style, but had blond hair and child-like brown eyes.

"Hello. I am Madame Elinor Chalamet and this is my apprentice, Mys Twyla Andricksson. We've just been admiring your artwork."

"I am Lady Ebbe Losendahl, and my friend is Mys Labrenda Elstad. Are you guests of the Creator?"

"Yes," I said quickly, before Twyla could say something to contradict me. "Is the Creator here now?"

"No. Maybe later. It doesn't matter really, does it, as long as we are all happy?" She shared a confiding smile with Labrenda and squeezed the dead girl's hand. The other did not speak, and I did not think she was human. She moved more like a doll than a living being, and her face had a lax passivity to its features.

At least Ebbe seemed to be alive. For the moment.

"Is Twyla your companion, Elinor?"

"No. Not in the way you mean. She is my student. I noticed there's an empty spot on one of your pedestals."

"Yes, that one is for me. Soon, my mortal self will take its place alongside the others, fulfilling the Creator's plan."

"Yes, the plan. The Creator's plan. Could you give me more details on that? I've forgotten some of it."

She gave a regal bow of her head, smiling. "Of course. Right now, I can only visit the Creator's kingdom when my body in the earthly realm is sleeping, but soon I will be here forever. Like the other Chosen Ones. Immortal. Never dying. Living forever." Her voice was dreamy and disconnected from emotion; somehow I didn't feel it was true to the person I had been told Ebbe was. How much of what she spoke of came from the drugs that were keeping her physical body enslaved?

"Where exactly will the ceremony be held? I don't want to miss it."

She didn't answer me but turned to go, her hand in Labrenda's as she glided away, much like a boat on a tide after it loses its mooring.

I called after her, "We are here because of your father, Baron Losendahl. He's very worried about you."

I was about to go after the two of them when Twyla, who had been remarkably silent during this exchange, tugged faintly at my sleeve. She said faintly, "Life is pulling me back. I can't hold us here any longer."

"What about Vonn?"

"After we came in here, I didn't feel him any longer." Her words were fading, and I had to strain to hear them. Her color was pale, her lips tinged with blue.

I put my arm around her waist, holding her up as her head rolled against my shoulder. "Take us home, Twyla."

～

As suddenly as we had appeared into the Beyond, we were back to the earthly plane. The shock of reality— the air moving against my face, the intense smells, the vibrant colors— slapped me brightly awake. Twyla was still in a swoon, and I gently laid her down on the couch, putting a pillow behind her head and back. She was semi-conscious, her eyelids flickering as she struggled to stay awake.

Anne-Marie was standing where we had left her, at the door with her hands still full of linens.

"Put that down, Anne-Marie, and fetch me a glass of sherry."

One thing about her, Anne-Marie was quick in an emergency. Without hand-wringing or asking a bunch of questions, in a flash, she returned with what I needed.

"You did well, Twyla. Now drink this."

There was a bit of sputtering, but she sipped, and the girl revived somewhat.

"What happened, Madame? One moment you were here, and then gone! Like a stage magician's act!"

"Our bodies weren't left here?" I said in surprise.

"No! Both of you vanished."

"Somehow, Twyla took both our corporeal bodies and souls to the Beyond." I shook my head. "Go to my cabinet and retrieve my pistol. Load it and bring it here, along with some extra bullets."

Anne-Marie's eyes practically popped from her head at my words, but she scurried to do as I asked. She returned and handed me the ammunition and the small pistol. Opening the chamber, I double-checked it was loaded before putting the gun in one pocket, the extra bullets in the other.

If Vonn came back, he was going to meet a different reception. He wanted to act as if he were alive? Fine. I would make him dead again.

"I want you to be extra careful, Anne-Marie. We have a malevolent ghost tracking us, and until I am sure he won't come here again, you need to stay on your toes. Don't ever be alone. I'll be requesting a guardia to stay here until we get this case resolved."

Anne-Marie nodded, her face solemn. Given the years she had been with me, she knew to take my warnings seriously.

"Call down to the kitchen and get an order in. Something hearty for Mys Andricksson, as she needs to renew her energy."

There was at least one advantage to draining yourself by contacting the spiritual world; you could eat to your heart's content and not gain weight. Or at least not too much. Anne-Marie left to our little kitchen, where a pull-button and a speaking horn should get us food soon.

Twyla was waking up, and she asked fearfully, "You don't think he'll come back, do you?"

"Don't worry about it. He won't be a problem soon. I plan on destroying his soul."

Twyla's eyes widened. What I referred to was the harshest penalty the Morpheus Society could give. The act of sundering took five Ghost Talkers to conduct the ceremony, for it needed the agreement and spiritual power of many. Sundering would mean that Vonn's soul would be destroyed, and any hope of moving from the Beyond to the Afterlife, gone. There would be no chance for salvation or atonement.

Chapter Fifteen

With Twyla settled, I wrote a brief note to Inspector Barbier requesting one of his men. Perhaps I wasn't thinking clearly, because this vague request for assistance brought down upon me a barrage of visitors. It turned out that when my request had arrived, Barbier had been closeted away with Archambeau and Baron Losendahl discussing the case.

"Please do be quiet! Mys Andricksson is asleep in my room, with Anne-Marie caring for her. I don't want them disturbed."

"Yes, let's be calm while we all hear the reason why you need guardia protection, madame," said the duke sarcastically. He was in one of his cold angers when his words sliced you like daggers.

Sensing a fight before I would give an explanation, Barbier said diplomatically, "I suggest we leave Dupont here with Mys Andricksson and your servant. Then we can adjourn to a private room to hear what has happened? Will that suit?"

I gave him a grateful smile. "Yes, please."

It was still a few hours before the fashionable dinner hour and Henri Colbert, the Crown's manager, easily found us accommodations in the same room we had used before. While the rest of us sat down at the round table, Archambeau remained standing, arms crossed, his eyes watching me as hard as slate.

The benefit to having all of them in one place was that I only had to tell my tale once. Our adventure was greeted by various degrees of shock and surprise among them, but my attention was only on Archambeau, whose expression grew harder with each word I uttered.

Inspector Barbier gave a low whistle. "Mysir Vonn? Who would have imagined we would need to deal with *him* ever again?"

I couldn't help but shudder.

Barbier asked, "How did he appear so real? Are you saying, Elinor, that he isn't dead?"

"No. He's dead, but like the ghosts at these parties, he appeared as if he were flesh. Perhaps he was one of the ghosts summoned before? We would need to ask Mysir Solberg." I gave the baron a sad frown. "If Vonn spoke the truth, he killed Hannah Wahl. He told us he found her in one of the alleys of the Hells and murdered her."

We were all silent for a moment, thinking of his last victim. For me, the fact that Ebbe had not asked after Hannah either showed she was not aware of her fate, or knew and did not care. I hoped it was the first.

I gave the baron the earring that had caused so much trouble. I had scrubbed away the blood that had gotten into the crevices of the diamond settings. The blood was probably why Vonn had found us so easily, since it tied the earring to his victim.

"Here is your daughter's earring. I did a brief cleansing ceremony with it, and it should be fine now. The other earring, I fear, is lost in the Beyond." I did not want to explain to him that it was a trophy kept by Vonn, so I left its whereabouts vague.

As he took it in his bear-sized paw, Baron Losendahl asked me, "You saw Ebbe? In this Beyond place? Yet you think she is still alive, not a ghost? I don't understand."

"Sometimes living beings get pulled into the Beyond. I've been there several times, but we can't stay long. Our vitality is anathema to the place of the dead. From what your daughter said, it seems her spirit travels there when she sleeps." I didn't add the word 'drugged'. He had enough to worry about.

Archambeau cut in. "You stated your servant said your physical bodies didn't remain on the earthly plane. That's different. Explain."

"I've never heard of that happening before, either. When a medium goes to the Beyond, it's through meditation, not through teleportation. It was something that Twyla made happen. When she revives, I will question her about it."

"You don't seem to know much."

Tired myself, I snapped back at the duke. "Do you want to hear what I do know, or are you going to loom over me? Questioning my every word as if I am the villain in this piece?"

Barbier once again stepped in as peacemaker. "Now, I'm sure we all want to hear what Elinor has to tell us. We can argue about what it means later."

Ignoring Archambeau's roll of his eyes, I said to the baron, "What concerns me is what your daughter tells me. We don't have much time before it might be impossible to bring her back. She clearly expects to stay forever in the Beyond, and I know no way of that happening without her death."

"Who is this Creator that Lady Losendahl mentioned? Is that Parnell Lafayette?" asked Barbier.

The baron was done with all of us. He pounded the table with his fist, demanding, "Where is my daughter?!"

Everyone reacted differently to the baron's pain. The inspector looked down at the notebook he held in his lap. The duke put his hand on his friend's shoulder, and I tried to offer some hope. "I've been thinking about where someone could hide a lady— or a group of girls, for we don't know how many he might have. A school for young ladies? A charity hospital? An asylum?"

"Too many to check in two days," said Barbier.

"What about the source of the drugs? Any luck there?"

The inspector shook his head. "Still checking that and the list we got from Lafayette."

"Twyla's research turned up the names of two missing girls, Lorraine Kaplan and Renee Bassett. They both went to the same lending library. We should check that out." I gave the name and location of it to the inspector, who jotted it down in his notebook.

After we had gone over everything at least three times, the meeting finally adjourned, with us no closer to linking Lafayette to any actual crime. Barbier agreed to my request for police protection, assigning Dupont and another officer to the task in alternating shifts. Tipping his hat to me, he said goodbye, promising to continue pursuing any possible lead.

Grief seemed to be shrinking the baron every time I met him. How I wanted to help him! And how frustrated I was at not being able to. He shook my hand goodbye. His wife was coming on the evening train, and he was meeting her at the station.

His departure left me alone with Archambeau.

"I will escort you back to your room, madame."

Back to being formal and stiff, were we?

The trip up the stairs was conducted in silence. Outside my door was Sergeant Dupont, a chair by his side for later repose. Giving him a passing glance, I didn't see any hint of intelligence, no matter how well hidden.

Archambeau followed me inside, probably so he could berate me for an incident I had no control over. As soon as the door was closed, I turned to face him, ready for battle.

"Do you have your gun?" was his first question.

I patted my pocket. "Of course."

I could tell he was doing his best to control himself, because his face was white and his eyes fiery. "Will you *promise* me not to hare off on your own? Or if you do, at least take Dupont. The man might be as bright as a potato, but at least he's a strong arm."

"What happened was not my fault," I insisted.

"Yet these things keep happening to you," he replied acerbically. "Perhaps it is because you go rushing off into danger without thinking? I thought you were one of the few women I knew that had a working brain, but I'm beginning to doubt that belief."

"I say that is unfair! What did you want me to do?"

Of course, he had no answer.

"Besides, who got me involved in this in the first place? You showing up at my door and simply asking Anne-Marie where I am, acting like no time has passed since we parted at Lindengaard. But I'm to jump into a carriage and run off to assist you like I'm your servant?! At your beck and call? Imagine if I arrived at your front door, demanding from your footman that I should speak to *you* immediately!"

He actually laughed, infuriating me further.

"I think Ruben would enjoy you visiting. I overheard him saying that Hartwood hasn't been exciting since you left."

He hadn't heard a word I said.

"You disappear for months with no word! I thought that, as friends, you might drop me a note. Perhaps arrange a meeting? But — nothing. Isn't that a little insulting?" To my own ears, my words acted like a flail against my raw feelings, and I cringed internally. It sounded so needy and desperate. A woman admitting she needed a man's attention!

His northern burr became broader, indicating his temper was not all quenched. "I had planned to do so, but was called away by the king on business. As I've explained."

"What a convenient excuse for rudeness! Thank you, Your Grace, for showing up and blessing me with your magnificence." I dropped a curtsy.

"Get up and stop speaking so foolishly," He snapped. "Stop calling me Your Grace in that supercilious way."

By this time, both of our voices were raised. I had forgotten about Anne-Marie and Twyla in the room next door. "Has it occurred to you that perhaps I do not appreciate being a tool to be used at your convenience?”

"If this investigation is too much for you, then bow out of it. Do not let me *inconvenience* you!”

"Of course I want to help! But, mannish, you twist my words around to win your argument.”

"And just like a woman, you want to hold the whip hand and make me jump at your command!” His hard breathing through his nose caused his nostrils to flare. Well, if I'd wanted my cold duke to warm up, he was blazing hot now.

We stared at each other, our chests heaving with emotion. For some reason, during our argument we had moved closer together.

"I do— do not— want you to jump at my command,” I said, almost crying with rage and other mixed emotions. "I was worried about you. Do you realize if anything happens when you are working for King Guénard, I might never know?”

His hand came up around my neck, under my hair, and he brought me even closer to him, his gaze holding mine. "As I am about you. Worried. Yes, I know this wasn't your fault, but please promise me to look after yourself?”

Looking up into his serious eyes, I said softly, "Do you think I'm some penny-paper heroine? That I'll go off with the villain and be tied to the railroad tracks until you rescue me in the nick of time?”

"So far, you seem to be determined not to be rescued. Stubborn woman. You keep saving yourself.”

"I do not think you would care for a woman who needed rescuing.”

"Perhaps, but occasionally a man wants a chance to be seen as his lady's champion. To remind her why she needs him around.” He gently brushed my hair from my forehead, tucking a long stray strand behind my ear. "You need to be more cautious. The world is a dangerous place, Elinor.”

"How dangerous?”

His hands on my temples, his fingers entangled in my hair, he closed the small space left between us as his warm mouth covered mine. We moved together in a synchronized dance of perfection.

Unfortunately, it was a bliss that could not last. When I opened my eyes, I saw over his shoulder the interested faces of my apprentice and servant through a crack in the bedroom door.

Chapter Sixteen

Sensing my distraction, Tristan looked over his shoulder and saw our audience just before they ducked back into the room.

"Madame, perhaps we can continue this conversation the next time we are truly private." With a bow, he left the room.

Hearing the front door, the two girls practically pushed each other out of the bedroom in order to surround me with their chatter.

"Wasn't that the Duke de Archambeau?" asked Anne-Marie with eager interest.

"You know it was!" said Twyla in a superior tone. "Imagine that! My mentor having an affair of the heart with one of the highest nobles of the land. Has he said he loves you? Have you exchanged tokens? Does he write you letters? Can we see them?"

"Please, Twyla! Please, just be quiet. And the answer is no to everything. This is not to be discussed at all."

Anne-Marie and Twyla exchanged looks. I had the sad feeling it was going to be discussed again, just not in my presence.

Trying to change topics, I said, "I'm glad to see you recovered, Twyla. How are you feeling?"

"Normal. I've already finished what Anne-Marie gave me. Is there anything else to eat? I'm starving!"

"Anne-Marie, show Twyla how to order using the speaking tube in the kitchenette. Get something for us all, including Sergeant Dupont, who is stuck on door duty."

The two girls went through the swing door and I heard Twyla asking Anne-Marie, "How long has Madame known the duke? Did you know they liked each other? How long have they been lovers? Didn't you know?"

Couldn't a woman have a moment to enjoy something of her own for a while? I collapsed onto the sofa, staring at the ceiling. Finding no answers written there, I picked up a book off the corner table. Trying to distract myself with reading was unsuccessful, for that moment with Tristan kept popping into my thoughts, breaking my concentration.

However, there was no time to savor it and wonder what Tristan had meant by his actions, for soon the two girls returned, carrying a tray of appetizers sent up in the dumbwaiter. After arranging it on a table, Anne-Marie went to close the drapes as the evening was starting to fall. Turning up the gas, she returned to where Twyla and I were starting to nibble on the crackers, cheese, and olives.

Before either of them could ask me anything intrusive, I went on the offensive.

"Tell me how you took us into the Beyond, Twyla."

"Oh, I've done that plenty of times. Whenever I wanted to get out of a boring class, I just left." She shrugged casually as I stared at her, shocked.

"Do you mean to tell me that you can leave the physical plane at any time and enter the Beyond?"

"Of course, I'm a natural. I told you that, remember? But I don't do it too much. It makes me tired and hungry." She buttered her third muffin and popped it into her mouth.

Anne-Marie quickly caught on that something unusual was

being discussed and inserted herself. "When I entered the suite, the three of you vanished. I thought I imagined it all. Is that unusual, madame?"

"Yes, very unusual. I don't know anyone else that can do that in the Morpheus Society."

"As I said, I have talents," Twyla said smugly.

I shook my head, trying to gather my thoughts. "Did no one at the Society tell you that couldn't be done? How unique it is? Who else knew you could do this?"

"No one else. I didn't tell anyone because I thought it would get me into more trouble. They were already mad at me for dropping plates and forgetting to turn off the bath taps."

Before I could question her further, I heard voices in the hall. It sounded like— but surely couldn't be— Parnell Lafayette!

"You two, get in the bedroom and this time stay there. Here, Anne-Marie, take the tray with you. And the cups. Be quiet in there, and no peeking."

After the bedroom door closed, I went to the front door and gently cracked it open. Yes, it was Parnell's voice. He was speaking with Sergeant Dupont. "—can't believe you're still with the inspector, Dupont. I was sure you wouldn't last."

Seeing me, my old school nemesis turned to me and removed his hat. "A word with you, Madame Chalamet."

"Certainly," I said, warily.

Stepping back from the open door, I let him enter. He barely glanced around the room before taking a seat, gesturing for me to do the same as if the place were his own. It gave me a strong desire to reach into my pocket for my man-stopper and shoot him.

"What brings you, Parnell? Not too busy draining the life force of young girls to visit?"

He didn't respond but started a speech that was clearly rehearsed. "It's come to my attention that you have an exceptional talent, Elinor. I would like you to consider using it to benefit all of mankind."

I blinked. That wasn't what I had expected.

"Exceptional talent? To benefit mankind? Whatever do you mean?"

He made a depreciating cough into his hand. "I see that in my eagerness to win you to my cause, I have not explained myself fully. A little bird in the Beyond has told me that you visited her with your apprentice. That your living flesh was able to maintain itself in the Beyond in a manner that I have not been able to do myself."

I made my face blank, hoping that the two girls would not crack open that door to listen in on what was about to be a very interesting and revealing conversation.

I said blandly, "You know the body cannot go into the Beyond, only the soul. Our spirit."

This close, I could see that the flesh was tightly stretched over his skull, his cheeks sunken, and his skin had a waxy sallowness to it. The man was definitely unwell.

He waggled a figure at me. "Don't be shy. We both know that isn't so. I designed my kingdom in the Beyond so only the living can enter. It is protected against the dead, otherwise ghosts would be wandering in and out of my domain. They litter the Beyond like pests."

"Naturally; it is their sphere."

"A sphere we should claim."

Thinking of Ebbe's companion, I said, "What of Labrenda Elstad? What is she? For she certainly is not alive!"

"A simulacrum. A construct. Elstad herself transitioned to the Afterlife long ago, but Lady Losendahl insisted she was the price for her cooperation in my experiment. So I showed her how she could shape whatever she wanted in the Beyond. That creature is simply a doll to bring comfort. Anything can be created in the Beyond by the living. You showed me that."

How I wish I had not!

"So you are the Creator Mys Losendahl spoke of?"

"Let me explain—"

"Please do."

He nodded to me, as though he was a king receiving a subject. "Did you ever wonder why mediums who have lost their minds in the Beyond appear younger than their true age? Why their faces have a cast of youth to them that does not fade away, no matter how many years pass?"

"If I had thought on it at all, I'm sure I would have concluded that it was their lack of wits which made them appear younger than their age. Just as a child's innocence makes them youthful."

"And there you would be wrong!" he exclaimed excitedly. His eyes flamed with feverish interest as he leaned over his knees as if to touch me. Thankfully, there was a span between us that didn't permit it. "It is because their minds wander in the Beyond! That is what keeps them young. The same energy that allows ghosts to exist for centuries in the Beyond flows from the medium's trapped mind backward into the body held on the Earthly plane."

"Interesting, but not really of value to those who cannot think or care for themselves without assistance."

Caught up in his own story, he barely paid my distaste at the idea any attention. "Now, think about this. What if the body and the mind could both go into the Beyond? To bathe themselves in the aura of a place halfway between earthly life and death?"

"Looking youthful? Is this what this is about? Taking girls like Lorraine Kaplan and Renee Bassett into the Beyond to do who-knows-what to appease vanity?"

"Mys Bassett is now an immortal. I've enshrined her pure essence to live forever," he said piously. "Unfortunately, Mys Kaplan was flawed. She could not understand the great honor she was receiving and left the project."

"Let me guess. She jumped— or was she pushed— in front of a train?"

Again, Parnell ignored what he didn't want to answer. "I used my mind, like you did fighting that ghost-dragon, to create my palace: a retreat on a scale as grand as a king's. In the Beyond, you are only limited by your imagination."

Not a very good one. He couldn't remember what his paintings should look like.

"Creating and maintaining are two different things."

"Just a minor problem. All it needs is enough energy, enough soul-spirit, and it will live forever in the Beyond. That will be fixed once my last disciple takes her final vows."

"In two days' time? During the full moon, I suppose?"

"The first night of the full moon is tonight."

At his words, I felt a desire to rush to the window to check the night sky. It took a lot of willpower not to do so.

"What I really came here to discuss with you is how you could help me. We are so close to learning the secret to never aging. Of stopping disease! Imagine, Elinor, a world where no one dies? My name— I mean, our names would go down in history as the ones to bring this great gift to mankind."

I wasn't going to waste time imagining any such thing. Instead, I was wondering when I should start shouting for Dupont to arrest him.

"You have the talent I need! It took months using volunteers before I was able to have both body and soul transported into the Beyond using my subject's dream-state. I must know how you do it!"

"First, tell me how you do it yourself. As a sign of good faith."

Since he thought I had my own method, Parnell confided in me. Or maybe it was just his need to brag that made him talkative.

"There is a halfway state, hovering between life and death, when the Beyond opens to the living. I give my subject a special drink I've concocted to open themselves up to these wonders." *I bet you do!* "Like a horse pulling a carriage, they bring me along with them. But while they can stay in the Beyond as long as they are in their trance, eventually I am pushed out. However, as each girl's spirit is enshrined forever in my palace, I gain the power to stay longer and longer."

And what of these girls enshrined forever?

"You are corrupting the nature of the Beyond! As you seek to live in a space never meant for us, do you realize that ghosts are becoming corporeal on the earthly plain? That they can now re-animate themselves here, not as spirits but as flesh and blood? It goes against the natural order of life!"

Perhaps he was too far into his madness to see my horror at his scheme, for he continued talking as if he had not heard my warning.

"Without the ritual preparation I've taken, it is impossible for the living to remain in the Beyond without inflicting damage upon yourself. Even Ebbe is starting to flag in her dedication, although I've increased the dose of what keeps her in the halfway state, hovering between life and death. That is why I'm here to see you."

"I don't understand."

"Ebbe told me you were there, inside my palace. Yet you appear so healthy, so vibrant, my dear Elinor. You must have exceptional spiritual strength. I must know your secret!"

For some reason, Parnell believed that it was I who had transported Twyla and myself to the Beyond. I put it down to his arrogance; he would never believe a mere apprentice had such a talent. To protect Twyla, I did not correct that notion.

"It was pure chance, Parnell. I doubt I could achieve it again," I said lightly. "One of your nasty ghosts, a well-known killer of girls in the Hells, showed up here, and I panicked. It simply happened; probably a dormant skill provoked by the need for survival."

"Yes, yes. That one has been a bother."

I said firmly, "Which is a good reason for stopping these experiments. Why don't you let me know where Lady Losendahl is? I'm sure the baron will provide you with a reward."

He pulled back, settling his shoulders against the high-backed plum-colored chair. Too late, I realized I had pushed him too hard.

"No. I think it would be better if you were to come with me, and I will exchange you for Lady Losendahl. You are worth more to me than an untrained girl obsessed with her dead friend."

I couldn't stop myself from laughing. "Really? That's your plan? That I take Ebbe Losendahl's place? No, thank you." His face flushed with anger; at least it gave some warmth to his skull-like face. "I think I'll call Sergeant Dupont in here to beat the information out of you."

"Lady Losendahl is in a heavily drugged state, at a location your pet gendarmes have not been able to find. Yes, I've seen them sniffing around. Without my appearance in the next hour to wake her, she will slip into a coma and die. Is that what you want? When just a little help from you could save her?"

For a moment I was tempted, but it would not do. This was an obvious trap, with my survival doubtful. "I'm sorry, Parnell, but I decline your offer to immolate myself."

Standing, I was ready to escort him to the door. He did not get up, but twirling his hat brim between his fingertips, said, "To sweeten my offer, I will give you information about your father's murder. You are still investigating that, aren't you, Elinor?"

Chapter Seventeen

His words froze me.

"What would you know of it? And why would I believe you?"

"Was I ever a liar? A braggart, perhaps, but I've never said anything that was untrue. Why would I be here, confident that I can convince you, unless I knew something of value? Such as the name of the man who killed Mysir Augustus Chalamet."

"You don't know it. You *can't* know it," I protested.

"Oh yes, Elinor, I've known for a couple of years now. The information came to me through an associate, the provider of that delightful concoction that puts my volunteers on the verge of death. The man doesn't know that I know, of course. Otherwise he might think of eliminating me, even though he benefits from my research just as much as I do."

I clenched my hands behind me to stop myself from launching myself at his face.

"I don't believe you. This is just some cruel joke of yours, on top of all the other twisted games you've played with these girls' lives. You've known since our training days my purpose in becoming a member of the Morpheus Society, and now you seek to use that to make me agree to this ludicrous plan of yours."

With that detestable wide grin, he stood up and made his way slowly to the door.

"Think on my offer, Elinor. Guide me for one final trip into the Beyond, where I shall stay forever, and in exchange I shall tell you the name of your father's killer. But the clock is ticking. Meet me at the Fontaine Park mermaid at midnight. I will bring Lady Losendahl, but you will bring no one."

"I will not agree to any of this until you can show me some proof that you know anything."

"Something that your pet police officer, Inspector Barbier, doesn't know? Well, Elinor, for you I shall share a little morsel. Mysir Chalamet was murdered because he knew of a greater crime and was about to speak of it."

"A greater crime? What crime?" I demanded. What did he know that I didn't?

He wagged his finger at me again. "If you wish to know more, you must agree to help me."

"I will do it, Parnell, but we will meet at one a.m. I have things to settle beforehand. Take my offer or not."

He nodded. "Till then."

After he left, I struck a match to a candle and placed the candlestick in the window. Anne-Marie and Twyla both emerged from the bedroom, speaking at the same time.

"You can't really be going, madame!" said Anne-Marie.

"So Mysir Lafayette is the one kidnapping girls? We should tell Sergeant Dupont." Twyla strode to the door.

"No. Come sit down and let us make a plan."

Twyla stood there, unmoving, her hand still outstretched toward the doorknob.

"Please, come sit down and let me tell you what I plan to do."

Reluctantly, she returned to take a seat next to Anne-Marie. Both were perched on the edge of their chairs.

"We have a couple of hours to think how we can handle this. If we go to the police or the duke, I am sure we shall never find Lady Losendahl." Twyla opened her mouth, but I put my finger over my lips to bid her to be quiet.

"But—"

"No buts. He will be on the lookout for anyone that looks like a guardia. The duke and baron are men who would be easily spotted. We shall use helpers Lafayette won't notice."

"You are thinking of Marcus," said Anne-Marie, who had noticed my signal placed in the window.

I nodded. "He and his fellows would be of great help. Hopefully, he will see the candle and join us soon."

"Marcus? The street rat who helped me find Hannah Wahl?" asked my apprentice.

"Yes. We've been friends for some years, and he knows how to move through the city better than anyone."

"If he's coming, I had better lay in more food," said Anne-Marie. She rose and went to place another order. My room service bill was going to be astronomical this month, especially as I no longer received a discount from the Crown in handling their Noise Ghost.

"But what shall I do?! I want to help!" wailed Twyla.

"You have one of the most important duties in the whole plan. If I get lost in the Beyond, you need to find me."

About half an hour later, Marcus arrived. At fourteen, he was going through a growth spurt and was starting to fill out a man's coat, though the arms were still a bit too long for his bony frame. He had a jaunty kerchief tied around his throat, its ends tucked down his shirt front as either an attempt at style or warmth.

"Madame," he said, shedding his cap. His eyes swiveled around casually, taking in Twyla, Anne-Marie, and everything else. I was sure he had just priced every knick-knack in the room.

"Thank you for coming at such short notice, Marcus. I hope you don't have any plans for this evening?"

"I took a pass on those opera tickets, madame, as soon as I got word about your light," he said, grinning. "You've got another job for me? Must be something special, it being this time of night."

While we were talking, I went to my desk and pulled out the flat bag where I kept my spare money. Counting out small bills until they made a stack, I rolled it and handed it to Marcus, who made it quickly disappear in some inner pocket that a cut-purse would never reach.

"What's this for? I haven't done anything yet."

"That's for finding the body of that young lady we were looking for. It is part of a reward that Baron Losendahl will give you in the near future. Tonight, I will shortly be meeting a gentleman in Fontaine Park at the mermaid statue. I want you and your friends already in place. The carriage I get into needs to be followed, and word sent back here about wherever it goes."

"That's all?"

"Of course, you can't be seen."

"If we don't want to be seen, we won't be seen," he said proudly.

"Good, because if you are, you risk my life." My melodramatic phrase, right out of the penny-paper adventures, evidently excited him.

Anne-Marie emerged with another tray of food from the Crown kitchens. I encouraged him to take what he wanted, and he stuffed his pockets while I told him the particulars of my plan.

"Remember, once you know where the carriage has taken me, you are to send word back immediately to Anne-Marie."

He nodded. One last apple going into another capacious pocket, he put his cap back on, sketched a dramatic bow, and left.

Now, I just needed to figure out a way of getting out of here without having Sergeant Dupont following me. For that, I'd need Anne-Marie's help.

About thirty minutes before I needed to be at the park to meet Parnell, Anne-Marie opened the door to the hall and told Sergeant Dupont that there was a rat in the kitchen.

"Come in and take care of it. Quietly, though, as madame and Mys Twyla are asleep in the next room."

From behind the door, hidden from view, I heard his big guardia boots stomp across the threshold. He paused just after entering the suite, and I had a view of his bull-sized back as he stood looking about, searching for the rodent.

"Over there. To the right is the kitchen door. It's in there. Catch it or kill it, I don't care, but it can't stay here."

Anne-Marie wasn't the best actress, for her voice showed no fear or trepidation. In reality she would have beaten such a thing with a broom herself, but Sergeant Dupont didn't know her, and he obediently went where her finger pointed.

As he disappeared through the swing door, I slipped out into the hall and made a quick race down the stairs to the lobby.

You could always rely upon finding a cab in the hotel district due to late-night parties, the theater, or the opera, which meant comings and goings at all hours. I dismissed two cab drivers as possibilities: one looked like a well-fed family man, and the other too nervous. The third man had a face that meant business, and I noticed a stout stick under his floorboard.

"I am meeting someone who might be unfriendly. Can you assist me?"

He tipped his hat, even as he asked, "In what way, madame?"

"He is to let a friend of mine return to the Royal Hotel in your cab, but he might prove obstinate about letting her go. Or have friends with him."

"No worries, madame. I'm always on the side of ladies in distress. And Bob, that's my horse, he won't let anyone catch us if we don't want them to."

I scrambled in and gave directions. It did not take us long, and once we reached the park, I paid my driver in advance, adding a substantial tip, as well as a folded note. Opening Father's watch, I saw I was a little early.

"When my friend is in the cab, please take her directly to the Royal Hotel and ask for Baron Losendahl. She is his daughter, and he will amply reward you if you give him this note."

"Will do, madame."

"You don't see any lurkers, do you?"

"Only a vagrant, and if he comes over here too close, I'll deal with him, ne'er you worry." The bat I had seen under his seat was now resting in his lap.

"Thank you."

We waited for another ten minutes before another carriage pulled up beside my own. Parnell leaned out from the door. "Get in."

I pulled out my man-stopper and pointed it at him. "First you give me Lady Losendahl. I've made arrangements with this driver to take the girl home to her father."

Parnell didn't look surprised. He would have been a fool not to expect something of this nature. Yet he was slow to respond, so I cautioned him. "This driver will go with the first sign of trouble, and your chance to convince me will be lost. Hurry up, Parnell, and give me Lady Losendahl."

He opened the door to his own carriage and helped Ebbe step out to the pavement. The girl's hair was a mess, trailing down her back, and her pale face was dazed and confused. She was in a rough way.

"Back away."

Parnell did so, hands raised, but with a mocking smile on his face.

I scrambled out and, taking Lady Losendahl by the arm, helped her into my quick-cab. "Step up." Child-like, she did as I bade, her face showing no recognition. Once I had her settled, I said to the driver, "Take her home."

"What about him?"

"No worries. I have friends, and this man cannot harm me."

He didn't look too pleased, but he snapped the whip over Bob's head and they clattered off, leaving me alone with Parnell Lafayette.

"The pistol, madame, or we go no further."

I took my thumb off the hammer and, reversing it, handed it to him.

"So far you've kept your bargain, but I warn you, Parnell, if you don't hold to the rest, you won't see the Beyond. I shall not cooperate, and you need my help. Desperately, don't you? You're dying, aren't you? That's why you want to live in the Beyond?"

"Yes. It's a disease attacking my nervous system. Similar to what Madame Granger suffers from, but worse. I shall be dead in a year, so you see, I have nothing to lose." He gave me a small, grim smile, his eyes flat and void of emotion. "Now, come along if you wish to learn the name of your father's killer."

Chapter Eighteen

I should have guessed. Of course Parnell was using the Morpheus Society sanatorium as his base. Well, I would kick myself later for being so stupid as not to consider the possibility.

The sanatorium was a five-acre estate on the outskirts of Alenbonné, where city life started to give way to that of a country village. It was designed to be a place of peace and quiet for those mediums who had lost their minds in the Beyond. Or those who needed physical recovery after arduous work.

At the approach of Parnell's carriage, the gates were swung open by two men, shadows without faces. Up the short drive, we pulled into the front of the building, parking at the portico. It had been a ladies' seminary before being bought by the Society, so had the feel of an institution. Very square and uniform in window placement.

Parnell did not help me down, and I was fine with not touching him. Inside, we were greeted by a middle-aged woman with pale blond hair streaked with gray. I did not recognize her.

"You poor dear," she said to me in a condescending manner,

before turning to Parnell and telling him, "I've prepared a room for her as you requested."

The whole set-up stank, but I reminded myself that I had agreed to this plan. I only needed to hold out until I was rescued.

Parnell's hand clamped vise-like onto my arm. Side-by-side, we went up the stairs and then down a long narrow foyer. There was a harsh smell of cleanser overlaying one of sickness and bodily smells of the worst kind.

The woman unlocked a room, handing the key to Parnell. "It's all yours. I've moved those in this wing to other accommodations so you can be private with your patient."

The sterile room inside was bare except for a hospital cot, a flat mattress, and a cabinet. The bed was that metal tubular type that can be cleaned quickly by staff and re-used for the next poor unfortunate. The shackles bolted to the wall on either side of the headboard didn't give me a feeling of trust.

Keep reminding yourself you have friends, Elinor. All will be well. Have faith.

"Make yourself comfortable while I mix my special drink for you, Elinor."

"First, tell me who killed my father."

"I've given you Lady Losendahl. Now it's time for you to hold to your part of the bargain. Bring my body and soul into the Beyond, and you'll learn the name. After all, Elinor, how many years have you waited? You can wait some more."

"If you know anything, tell me now. I'm in your power, after all."

Still, he said nothing. I caught the whiff of licorice. With his back to me, he measured his filthy drink.

"Tell me, or I won't help you."

He turned and said with detached interest, "Did you know your father knew his killer? That the two had made a private arrangement to discuss the matter of a theft that had taken place earlier that year? You see, dear Elinor, certain gems came through your father's hands from a robbery and he immediately recognized them to be stolen. Stupid of the thief not to realize your father would recognize them, even if they had been removed from their settings. But he was new to his criminal career back in those days. He would not make that mistake today."

He brought the metal goblet over to where I sat on the bed.

"I give you this information to prove that I do know more. But if I give you his name, my life would be worth nothing. So I shall give you that information only when I am safely in the Beyond, far away from him and his network of brigands. Drink, Elinor, and let us go to the Beyond together."

The smell of the drink made my stomach pitch. *Calm down. I can do this. I've been to the Beyond plenty of times.* This would be no different. Stalling, I asked, "How does this work exactly?"

"You take this like a good little girl, and soon you will find yourself in the Beyond, in a halfway state between life and death."

"It's the dead part I have a problem with. It doesn't encourage me to take the plunge, Parnell."

"Strictly a temporary state, I assure you. Or you could just transport us both to the Beyond? Like you did before?" he suggested.

"I told you, I didn't do that consciously. It must have been a survival tactic when I was faced with that murderer Vonn."

His eyes had a very unpleasant gleam to them. "Perhaps when you start to dream, it will come back to you? Regardless, your spiritual vigor will become mine, something I treasure far more than Ebbe Losendahl's tedious wish to be reunited with her dead school-chum."

He held up the chalice and viewed it speculatively. "It seems poetic to me that the woman who was a thorn in my side throughout my time in the Society will now be the instrument of fulfilling my dearest dream— to live forever in my own kingdom, finally vanquishing death. When Ebbe told me you had visited, it seemed a golden opportunity of making *you* the instrument allowing me immortality."

Parnell handed me the chalice, and I took it in cold hands.

"Now, drink up, Elinor, and we will both have what we desire above all else."

Taking a deep breath, I swallowed it down in one long gulp.

As I succumbed to the drug on the earthly plane, Parnell whispered in my ear what to do: imagine myself back in the Beyond, in his palace. As I formed the image, I would find myself there. Then, picture him in the flesh and so he would become one.

Before I did anything like that, I wanted to make sure nothing of Ebbe Losendahl remained in his kingdom. Exploring the place, I eventually found myself in the same hall of statues. Some rags on the floor drew my attention; it was only as I approached that I realized I had found Labrenda Elstad.

I approached cautiously to find her body as flat and rumpled as a discarded dress. The doll lay on the floor, a discarded husk of a plaything with blank eyes and a sunken face. It did not stir when I called out its name or when I touched it with my shoe.

Swallowing hard, I turned my attention back to Parnell's statues, examining each closely. They were lifelike in form and held the beauty of an ice sculpture, frozen. I reached up and hesitantly touched the skirt of one, and again felt that jumping tingle through my fingertips that jolted me all the way to my spine. Keeping my hand in place, I realized there was no feeling of personality, of soul, but only of energy.

Somehow, Parnell had sorted these girls like wheat from chaff, keeping only what he needed to power his dream place. There was nothing left that was them.

"Elinor, Elinor Chalamet. Let me in, I command you."

Parnell's whispers swirled all around me. "Elinor, Elinor Chalamet. Let me in!"

He must be applying some force, because I was finding it harder to concentrate without his voice intruding. It was time to find out the name of my father's killer. After all, wasn't that the reason for risking myself?

Placing in my mind's eye how he looked, I started shaping an image of Parnell Lafayette: the scholarly, skull-like face, the skin the color of old beeswax, and the hunched body emaciated by illness. The domed head and its thin, blond hair. The bitter lips, almost colorless, and the long slope of his nose.

"Good, Elinor! I feel your power. So much more than poor Ebbe! You have made me flesh!"

I had indeed done as he requested, and my adversary now stood in front of me, solid as life— with one notable exception. It took a moment before he realized it.

"Why is it so dark here? Where are you, Elinor?"

"I'm here, Parnell, as you are. I fulfilled my promises, but I never agreed to give you eyes."

He screamed. "Make me whole, Elinor Chalamet, or you will learn nothing!"

Parnell blundered into the bases of the statues, his arms flailing out in front of him, searching for me. I easily dodged out of his way as we weaved in and out of the statues of his other victims. He tripped over the crumpled thing that had been Labrenda Elstad and stepped on her face, making my stomach give a dry heave.

"Give me my eyes! My eyes!"

"You may have me trapped on the physical plane, Parnell, but here in the Beyond I am mistress. Tell me who killed my father, or end up being a blind immortal. Forget finding yourself some other girl to victimize. I imagine the Duke de Archambeau and Inspector Barbier are already on their way to the sanitorium."

He hit one statue too hard. Reeling backward with his hand on his forehead, he muttered savagely, "You'll pay for this."

"Tell me who killed my father."

But once again, I had pushed him too far. He was too angry, too malicious to give in to a mere woman. I felt a change in the energy of the Beyond; a breeze on the back of my neck made my spine shiver.

"You want to play games, Elinor? Enjoy this one. I have opened a door to my palace and let Vonn inside to hunt you. Remember, when he kills your soul in the Beyond, your body will remain forever in the sanatorium, as witless as all the others."

I had no time to respond, because Parnell's projection winked out; he had cut our connection and returned to the earthly plane.

"We meet again, my lovely," said the killer of Hannah Wahl.

Keeping one of the statues between me and him, I tried leaving the Beyond and returning to my body, but the drug kept me here.

"Pretty lady," said Vonn, giving me a savage grin. "Will you rip as good as the other girl?"

He kept making horrible comments about what he'd do to me while I tried to make some sort of plan. With ghosts, there was only one option for utterly destroying them: a sundering, the plan I had told Twyla I would enact. But for a sundering, I needed five Ghost Talkers to agree to destroying his soul. Five could bring the energy needed to sentence such evil. And I was by myself. Or was I?

These statues, their essences... could I use them? Could I tap into their power and harness it?

Touching the one Twyla had named as Renee Bassett, I put my palm flat on the hem of her dress and summoned. The energy unraveled so quickly that I jumped back as the statue shattered, pieces of marble cracking apart to fall on the ground, revealing a shimmering pillar of white-hearted blue flame.

"What are you doing, witch?! It won't save you!" yelled Vonn.

I had no time to think. If he reached me with that knife, my soul would be done. I rushed to the next statue to see if I could duplicate my success.

The next statue burst like a dried husk, the marble splitting in half so the front part of her form slid to the ground. It landed face up, as if the girl herself had swooned to the floor. On the plinth, all that was left was another white-hearted blue flame, as tall as the statue that had fallen.

I had never seen anything like it before, but there was no time to stare in wonder. Vonn was screaming. I broke the third of the five statues, the world that Parnell Lafayette had created from his mind began to fall apart.

The roof shuddered, plaster dust falling down into my hair. Above me were now black and gray storm clouds filled with flashes of lightning. Like everything in the Beyond, there was no smell of a storm, no sound of thunder, only the semblance of reality.

"Stop what you are doing!"

Of course, I did not. I had four flames now. The thunderstorm moved lower, the lightning striking the walls, blasting them away in soundless explosions to reveal nothing behind them but mist.

Vonn moved to the last statue, blocking me. His knife slashed out, and I felt it slide along my dress, splitting the fabric and leaving a streak of red down my arm. The pain was indescribable. It scorched me from heart to brain, leaving a trail of fire that burned my being like acid. Instinctively, I covered the wound with my other hand.

I brought the four pillars of flame together, molding their energy into mine like clay. To sunder a soul was not to be undertaken lightly; the process had been known to kill those who tried it. I was past caring. It would need to be done now. There was no going back.

Everything around me was shaking into pieces, including me. My head felt like it was going to be split apart. As each girl's soul was bound, their name was given to me: Renee Bassett, Louisa Bonnet, Meike Roord, and Frida Korver. Yet I felt no personality, no thoughts, just raw power.

Winding them together, they made a pillar of white-yellow

light. As the column turned, it spiraled upward into the storm clouds. It attracted lightning.

When a bolt struck it, it sent a trail of fire all the way back down to the ground. It shattered the earth under me, and unable to stand, I fell backwards, flailing, into the void.

~

I awoke lying on a hard surface. I rolled up and brought my knees to my chin, staring into nothingness. Parnell Lafayette's palace was gone. No longer having his victims in place to serve as fuel, it had shattered like a cracked egg. It was lost, as was I.

Immediately my mind tried to form a landscape, a place, something, but I was too tired, utterly spent. All my energy had been tapped to evict Vonn from the three planes of existence: the earthly, the Beyond, and the Afterlife.

At least I had the satisfaction of knowing that the creature was no more.

Feebly, I reached for the tie that connected the soul to the physical body, and found nothing but a broken thread. Was this due to Vonn's attack, or had Parnell killed my earthly form? I did not know.

But as I climbed to my aching feet, I didn't feel like a ghost. Surely I was still flesh somewhere? Although perhaps all ghosts felt that way. Thinking of that made my skin crawl. If I got back and had a chance to discuss such things with any future spirits I encountered, I would ask them about it. For now, I just wanted to return to where I belonged.

Where was Twyla? I had asked her to find me in the Beyond, to help bring me back, but clearly something had gone awry with that plan. Perhaps I could summon her instead? I called. Nothing.

I was a guttering candle. Tears slipped from my eyes, for the pain from the soul wound ached in ways that I could not describe.

The pain was like nothing I had ever experienced before, and it drained my ability to think clearly.

My plans to protect myself had failed. Tristan would probably enjoy giving me a lecture about my stupidity, if I ever made it back.

Thinking of him— his face, how he moved and talked— something in my heart trembled, awakening, putting out a call that was like a summoning, but so much more. As it stirred, something in the distance swirled, changing to a lighter shade of gray. I started walking towards it, and around me with each step a scene took shape, like under a painter's brush. Colors of green, blue, and white became shapes.

Suddenly, I was on a hillside and it was summer, for the grass was lush and wildflowers of white, yellow, and blue brushed against my skirts. Past the meadow was a conifer forest, and further away in the distance were mountains capped in snow.

This landscape was not from my mind, for I had never seen such mountains. I reached down to pluck one of the flowers, but it passed through my hand, disappearing. It was an illusion. I was in someone's created place. A dream place for a ghost?

Now I saw her— surely the most beautiful woman in the world. Thick black hair that, unbound, whipped around her head with the wind that was rising. Even from where I stood, I could see her eyes were of that light emerald that in gemstones is highly prized. Thick black eyelashes accented the shape of her eyes, making them appear even larger and more brilliant in color. An oblong face with a high forehead, a straight, perfect nose, and a naturally red mouth which was just the right size to be sultry, made up her face.

She was tall, and her figure was a natural hourglass; she wore a dress of dull gold, and over it a heavy coat in red.

Even when screaming, her voice was beautiful: thick and sweet, like being drowned in honey.

"Kill me! You've always wanted me dead! Do it, if you aren't a coward!"

"As you wish, Minette," said Tristan Fontaine, the Duke de Archambeau.

Suddenly, I realized that he was standing to my right in a white flowing shirt, half tucked into his tan riding breeches. While he wore tall riding boots, he looked as though he had dressed hastily, for his hair was unkempt and that hard jawline of his had a shadow of a beard.

Tristan raised his right arm, his hand holding a dueling pistol. When it went off, the sound was so loud I covered my ears. Ten yards away, Minette fell gracefully to the ground in a heap, dead.

Tristan turned to me, lowering his arm.

"I killed her. I'm a murderer," he said flatly.

"Hm. Yes. Well, enough about that. I'm lost in the Beyond, and really need your help getting out of here."

The dreamy expression on his face grew harder, more intelligent. Life awoke in his dream manikin. "What? What are you doing here? You're never in these dreams."

I reached out and shook his arm. "Listen to me. You're probably about to wake up, and I need you to remember this. Go to Twyla. Find Anne-Marie. Tell them my body is at the institute run by the Morpheus Society. You need to hurry! Will you remember? Will you remember? Will you remember?"

My voice echoed as the dream disintegrated away, leaving me alone in the gray formless Beyond.

Chapter Nineteen

This is what Twyla later related:

There's so much to tell you! I'll just start at when you left, and if I skip anything you want to know, interrupt me.

Sergeant Dupont didn't complain about not finding the imaginary rat, he just returned to his post at the door. He's a proper dunce! So slow!

Anne-Marie and I played cards while we waited. She is either very good at playing Dead Man's Noose, or she knows how to cheat. I don't know which, but I suspect the latter. I'm going to ask her to show me how she does it.

Hours passed, and when we didn't hear from Marcus we both wondered what we should do. But then, who should burst through the door? The Duke de Archambeau!

He was shouting at the top of his lungs, with Sergeant Dupont trailing behind, hanging his head. "Where is she?" he demanded.

I started explaining but he just grabbed me, shaking me so hard my teeth hurt.

"Stop your babbling and let Anne-Marie tell me!"

He didn't act very lover-like. There was nothing weepy or

hand-wringing about him, even though you were in danger. If he does send you a love note, does it begin with 'troublesome woman'?

"What was Elinor thinking? To put herself in that man's hands! I knew this would happen. Next time, I shall lock her in a cell and throw away the key!"

Anne-Marie tried to reassure him, but to no avail.

"Marcus will send word back on where she is."

He gave her such a look!

"I know where she is. She's in the Beyond. She sent me a message and told me to contact Mys Andricksson. That you would be able to rescue her. Stop blubbering and do it now. At once!"

I tried, madame, I really tried. First I looked for you in Parnell's palace, that strange place where we met Lady Losendahl, but I came up empty. It had vanished or was so well-hidden I couldn't locate it. Next, keeping my thoughts focused on you, I tried to summon, but again, nothing responded to my call.

Before His Grace could shake me again, one of the street imps showed up. It was a dirty little girl dressed in soiled boy clothes, and on her head was perched what I thought was a bird's nest only to realize later it was actually her hair.

When he realized she had a message from Marcus, he shook her too! It seems he thinks shaking people makes them think. The poor thing went mum, her terrified eyes as big as saucers. It took some cajoling by Anne-Marie, who gave her a cookie and her prized newsboy cap, to get the child to speak.

"Marcus told Jenny, who told Johann, who sent a message to Aaden, that the prize you be looking for is at the madhouse. The place the ghost folk are sent when their minds go to pudding."

I explained what she meant. "She means the institute. I know where it is."

"Elinor already told me where she was," he snapped back. "Since you cannot help her from here, we shall go and demand some answers there."

He started barking orders at us. "Anne-Marie, send a note to Inspector Barbier to meet us there. Then stay here in case there is any more news or messages. Sergeant Dupont and Mys Andricksson, with me."

The duke's carriage was waiting for us outside, and his horses galloped so fast I had to grab the strap to keep my seat while His Grace interrogated me about the sanatorium. He wanted to know about the property and the layout of the building. Who might be there. How heavily it was guarded.

The carriage pulled around to a side lane, passing the locked gates. The wall was not very tall, and with the duke giving him a leg up, Sergeant Dupont was able to lurch his hefty backside over it. I thought His Grace was going to leave me behind, but I told him I'd scream if he did. And I can scream very loud.

He was surprised not to find dogs on the property, but I told him that they couldn't have dangerous animals running around when patients might wander away. Besides, it wasn't a prison!

"Then why are the gates locked, Useless?" asked His Grace.

"It's the middle of the night!" I reminded him.

He told the sergeant to enter the back of the building where the kitchens and dining hall were located. The duke himself had other plans.

"We're going to walk right in?" I asked, surprised by his audacity.

"Yes."

He didn't wait for me, but started up the main path. I had to trot to keep up. When we entered the institute, an old lady was at the front desk. She was surprised to see us, alarm plain on her face.

"Excuse me, but these are not visiting hours. You can come back later in the morning, after ten, to see a patient or visit with a doctor."

I blurted out before the duke could speak, "I'm Mys Twyla Andricksson, here to visit my mentor, Madame Elinor Chalamet. I think she's here?"

She clucked her tongue. "That doesn't give an apprentice permission to come barging in here in the middle of the night. We have schedules here!"

"I'm sorry," I said, trying to act humble. "Is she here?"

The night manager grumbled, but after taking forever to check her ledger she finally said, "I don't see that name. You must be mistaken."

I looked sideways at the duke. His face was like one of those horrible storms that blows into the harbor and breaks the masts of ships. He said, "We've been told by Mysir Parnell Lafayette that she is here. Perhaps we can speak with him?"

Under the desk I saw her fingers move, pressing something. I had no time to warn His Grace because in a moment we were faced with two men who came out of the rooms behind her. Thugs. Big and broad, with a look that meant business.

"Escort these two—"

She didn't even get the words out before the duke grabbed a chair from the entry hall and, in a swift lunge, knocked it flat against the face of one man. As the other charged us, the duke feinted to the right, before abruptly changing direction to the left. As the man went by him, he smashed the oak frame against the top of the brute. He went down to join the other crumpled on the floor.

Was it wrong that I jumped up and down and clapped? Finally he was showing some lover-like spirit!

The woman was about to run, but the duke caught her by the wrist and in a flash he had her arm twisted high behind her back. He had no sympathy for her sex, and his fierce growl was not one I would like directed at me. "Where is she?"

From the top of the stairs, Mysir Lafayette said, "Stop abusing my poor staff, Your Grace. If you want answers, ask me."

Lafayette was pointing a pistol at us! The duke pulled the woman in front of us like a shield, causing her to beg Lafayette to put away his weapon, while His Grace commanded me to get behind him. I jumped to do so.

We did not stay in the foyer long. His Grace shoved the struggling woman in front of him up the staircase. We started climbing upward, towards Lafayette. The old lady continued going on about how everyone should remain calm. I thought the duke was being amazingly calm, myself!

Lafayette kept talking. "If you don't leave now, you'll never see Elinor again. Unless it's at the morgue."

By this time, we were near the top of the landing and Lafayette backed away from the railing. I'd swear the hand holding the pistol was actually shaking. Not a very brave man, Elinor. Not like the duke.

"Where is she?" His Grace demanded again.

"She came willingly."

"Where is she?"

"Stop moving! Do you think I will not shoot?"

Crouched behind the duke's back, I could not see his face, but I could feel the taut muscles under his coat. He was about to make a move. One of his hands came behind him and tapped me, pointing to the side where there was a potted plant. I tapped back on his hand to let him know I understood.

We were of one mind! We were both determined to save you!

I jumped sideways and threw myself at the pot, sending the plant toppling. It made me fall down a few stair steps, so I grabbed the railing to stop my descent.

The pistol went off, but the shot must have gone wide, for when I opened my eyes, the duke had Lafayette's neck in his grip and was shaking him so vigorously the man's feet came off the floor. Like I said, His Grace does like shaking people!

"For the last time, where is she?"

"I don't have to answer."

His Grace took the small finger on Lafayette's right hand and brought it backward, toward his wrist. We all heard the snap. The man gave a high-pitched howling scream. I might have given a sympathy scream at the same time.

"That's one." If Lafayette was going to speak, he didn't get a chance, because the duke said, "Two." There was another snap. "Now, *where is she?!*"

Perhaps the manager didn't like to hear snapping finger bones either for she screamed, "Down the hall! In the last room."

Grabbing the pistol off the floor where Lafayette had dropped it, His Grace brought the butt down on the man's temple. Lafayette went down, moaning. His Grace left him like discarded trash, and stalked down the hall. I ran after him.

"Hold this." He handed me Lafayette's gun, and it was only then that I recognized that it was your own dear man-stopper! The cad! Taking a gun from a woman! I gripped the handle as hard as I could so I wouldn't drop it.

His Grace brought the heel of his boot down so hard to the left of the doorknob that the wood splintered. A second blow and the door gave way. Inside we found you, unconscious on a bed.

I couldn't look away! It was like the best part of a play! He had you in his arms and made all sorts of promises and so many endearments! Here— I've written it all down for you so you can put it under your pillow to dream about. He was very gushy until he noticed I was watching. Then he told me to save you or he'd pull my skin inside-out through my nose.

It was your father's watch, in your pocket, that I used to locate you in the Beyond. It showed me where you were, just like a compass.

Chapter Twenty

Remembering took energy, and that I had little enough of as I lay in a nice soft bed. While I was no longer drugged, the room kept moving around me at odd moments, and lifting a hand to hold a spoon to my mouth took a great deal of will-power. Overall, I felt very tired, with no motivation to stay awake.

Anne-Marie helped me bathe in the huge bathtub with the gold-plated faucets. With my head resting on the tub's rim, she tried brushing out my hair. "It's horribly matted."

"Is it?" I asked, floating among the bubbles. "Just cut it off, then."

"Never!" said Anne-Marie, shocked. "I'll put some nut oil into the knots and then use a comb. The knots will work out, you'll see."

I was dozing by the time she was done, and the bath water had long grown cold.

"Here." She wrapped me in a towel, nice and fluffy, and helped me back to the bed. A nightgown was tugged over my head, and I was sandwiched between sheets that smelled of oranges and basil. Between one blink and another, I was asleep.

It was almost impossible for me to sort out the days. At some time Charlotte showed up, her concerned face floating into my waking dreams.

"You need to get up and move around. Drink a lot of water. To get the drugs out of your system."

I nodded my head obediently, my thoughts still floating above my body. With Charlotte grabbing one arm and Anne-Marie the other, they pulled me to standing and made me walk the length of the room. My legs bent from under me, and without their support I would have fallen to the floor.

"Come on, Elinor, help us help you," Charlotte begged and coaxed.

I tried, I really did, but the walk didn't take long to wind me. Back under covers, a tray sitting on my lap, they force-fed me bone broth. After I spilled most of the stuff, Anne-Marie took the spoon from my hands and worked on getting me to take it.

Sleep, eat, sleep, until eventually I was able to hold my own spoon, and I spent more time awake with a headache than asleep, knowing nothing.

Watching Charlotte, who was sitting in a chair near the window, reading, I asked, "Where am I? This isn't the Crown."

"It's the duke's town home. Hartwood."

"Why am I not at the Crown?"

"He didn't trust you to be protected at the Crown. That's what he told me. After all that's happened, I'm not surprised that he's being careful."

"What do you mean?"

She set aside her book and gave me her full attention. "I was wondering how long it would take you to ask. Not a good sign that you weren't curious about it all. Not the Elinor I know."

She came over to where I was sitting up, mounds of pillows behind me. Instinctively, her hand went immediately to check my pulse. Looking at my own arm, I was surprised to see no wound, only a long white scar on my forearm. From the way it ached, I had expected to see a bandage.

"Tell me."

"First, your kidnapper? Parnell Lafayette? Killed himself by leaping over the balcony at the sanitarium right after they found you. Or at least that's what Sergeant Dupont says is what he saw happen. He was standing over Lafayette when Barbier found them."

"You don't think Barbier is covering things up? Tristan didn't—?"

"No. Your apprentice swears they left Lafayette alive on the first floor with two broken fingers and a sore head, but that was it."

"What about that woman who told them where I was?"

"Gone. Vanished. No one can find her."

My head hurt too much to figure it all out. "Go on. What else did Twyla not tell me?"

"Everyone's guess is that Lafayette couldn't take the disgrace. Doing the autopsy, I found his body riddled with disease. He didn't have much longer to live. The Morpheus Society disavows him, and Madame Granger is cleaning house with a vengeance. Seems the old lady can stir herself when required, especially when she fears the king might dissolve her mystical group if action isn't taken."

"What about Parnell's research? Surely he left notes."

"Inspector Barbier found burned papers in the fireplace grate of his office. Could be Lafayette destroyed them, or one of his employees didn't want to be blamed for keeping a noblewoman against her will. I suspect it was that woman at the sanatorium. Whoever did it, they conducted a clean sweep through his office and home."

"And Ebbe?" I asked faintly.

From her expression, I knew the news would be bad. "She's awake, Elinor. But I don't think she'll regain her mind. Lady

Losendahl takes simple commands and is obedient to whatever you ask, like a child, but the spark of independence? Intelligence? I don't see it. Her parents hold out hope, though, and maybe time will heal her."

I sighed. She was one of the things I had lost. The other was my faith in the Morpheus Society— along with part of my soul. I wasn't sure which hurt the most.

"Thank you, Charlotte."

"Think nothing of it. Besides, it gets me out of the morgue."

As I gained more strength, it became inevitable that I would eventually have a meeting with the Duke de Archambeau. I had graduated from the bed and was sitting in the conservatory when he arrived, unannounced.

He sat down next to me, and I said what was expected. "I want to thank you—"

Tristan cut me off. "Your rescue is down to your own actions."

I bowed my head in contrite agreement. "I think you played a part in it."

Wondering what else I could say that wasn't about Lafayette or Tristan's murdered wife, I asked, "When is your family returning?"

"In another week."

"I wanted you to know I've made arrangements for other accommodations. Charlotte has arranged a rest cure with a doctor friend of hers."

"Hm." His face was inscrutable. What he was thinking, I could not guess.

I set my book aside on the table. It had not been holding my attention, anyway.

He reached into an inner pocket and withdrew a soft brown leather pouch. "I have something for you to see that I think will interest you."

I reached out my hand, but he dropped the pouch into my lap instead. Loosening the drawstring, I shook out the contents, and out poured a collection of sparkling gems. My hands couldn't help themselves; they caressed the precious gemstones.

"Spoils from that case I am working. They were found in a blackmailer's safe."

My mind leapt to the only blackmailer I knew. "Lord Buckard?"

"No. But it was someone known to him. Remember my master criminal?"

"You've caught him?"

"No. Not yet. It seems Buckard was just a small spider on a rather large web, but he gave me information about another who had a safe with these gems and missing government correspondence."

I held one of the gemstones up to my naked eye, letting the light catch it. From his vest pocket, Tristan pulled something else and handed it to me.

"Anne-Marie loaned me your jeweler's loupe for you to use."

Opening the hinge to reveal the magnifying lens, I held it to my eye. "A very nice diamond. Authentic and high grade."

Something about its old-fashioned cut seemed familiar. *Ah.* Yes, it was the right size and shape to fit a necklace I had seen at the Hartwood dinner party my first time here.

"Lady Baudelaire's necklace that she wore at your dinner party during the Monet case. The one gifted to her husband's ancestors. Do you remember it?"

"Yes, it's one of her favorites to wear. Why?"

"The centerpiece was a jewel with this exact same cut. Not a common one nowadays, as it doesn't reflect the light as well as newer methods used to shape a stone."

Tristan bent over to look more closely at the gem I held. "You mean this is a copy?"

"No. I mean this is the real stone, and the one she wore was false. When I saw it, I felt sure the stones were replicas. It is some-thing rich people do: get copies made so they can wear their precious pieces safely, without the risk of them being stolen or broken." I put the stone back in the pile. "I would talk with her. She may be more forthcoming to you about how the gem ended up with your blackmailer."

There was a good mix of precious and semi-precious: diamonds, rubies, emeralds, along with sapphires, and tourmaline. I kept picking them up, examining them under the magnifying glass.

I froze.

Tristan must have detected the change in my manner, for he asked quickly, "What is it?"

My fingers were shaking as I took a deep breath. I looked again. There was no doubt of it.

"This ruby has a distinctive occlusion. I know it. My father had it in his workshop right before he died. It was one of the items stolen from him."

Parnell had told me the truth. It was all connected. The master criminal that Archambeau hunted was my father's killer.

Find more great reads
by Byrd Nash
at her website
ByrdNash.com

Author Notes

I've always been fascinated by ghosts and have wanted to write a story about them for some time. Pair that with a longstanding love of Sherlock Holmes, that started when I was about nine, and you have the Madame Chalamet series.

My editor, Emma, worked hard by asking all the right questions. As always some great Beta readers helped to shape up the story: Amirah, Davida, and Laurie.

Thank you to the readers who have been so enthusiastic about this series. I appreciate all your feedback on Elinor!

BYRD NASH

NOTE: This fantasy world is inspired by 1910 France, but is not a part of it.

For convenience sake, American spellings have been chosen for this fantasy series. For example, instead of grey, gray is used.

For use in this fantasy world, Guardia refers to an individual police officer. Gendarmes to the police force, or a group of police officers.

Cast of Characters

- **Elinor Chalamet** (Shall-ah-may)— A Ghost Talker residing in the city of Alenbonné (Alan-bon-ay) in the country of Sarnesse (Sar-nessie).
- **Tristan Fontaine** Duke of Archambeau (Are-shem-bow)— is a member of Alenbonné nobility, **Le beau idéal**. For simplicity, duke is only capitalized when it is used with his title, either Duke de Archambeau or Duke de Chambaux (province title).

Tristan's circle:

- **Baron Viktor Losendahl**— a friend of Tristan's who's daughter, Ebbe, is missing. A native to Zulskaya.
- **Minette Fontaine**, the previous Duchesse de Chambaux (deceased)— wife of Tristan.
- **The Duchesse de Chambaux** (Sham-beau)— Tristan's mother.
- **Lady Valentina Fontaine**— Tristan's sister.
- **Lady Josephine Baudelaire** (Bowed-lair)— a society lady who was a friend of Minette's and the Chambaux family.

Elinor's connections:

- **Twyla Andricksson**— Elinor's apprentice, assigned to Elinor by Parnell Lafayette.

- **Parnell Lafayette**— a high ranking person in The Morpheus Society whom Elinor knew when she was in training to be a medium.
- **Leona Granger**— Elinor's mentor in The Morpheus Society.
- **Jacques Moreau** (More-row)— a childhood friend of Elinor's who is now a soldier.
- **Dr. Charlotte LaRue** (Lah-roo)— the city's coroner and university instructor, and a friend of Elinor's.
- **Inspector Marcellus Barbier** (Bahr-bee-er)— a police inspector who Elinor works with to solve crimes.
- **Sergeant Quincy Dupont** (Dew-pon)— Barbier's subordinate.
- **Augustus Chalamet** (deceased)— Elinor's father who was murdered about 12 years ago at the start of Ghost Talker. He was a well-known jeweler to the king and nobility.

Ebbe Losendahl's Circle:

- **Karl Solberg** — Ebbe's male acquaintance who has a wandering eye.
- **Hannah Wahl**— Ebbe's very pretty maid
- **Elyna Hummel**— Ebbe's school friend.
- **Lisette Paquet**— Ebbe's school friend.
- **Labrenda Elstad**— Ebbe's school friend who died in a tragic accident.

Servants and Helpers:

- **Anne-Marie**— Elinor's servant, a daughter of a sailor.
- **Marcus**— an orphaned street urchin who occasionally helps Elinor.

- **Madame Travers**— a strong-minded upper housekeeper at the Royal hotel.
- **Ruben**— a footman in the de Chambaux household.
- **Madame Darly**— the duke's cook at his townhouse, Hartwood.

Ghost Theory & the Morpheus Society:

- **The Morpheus Society**— an intellectual group of amateurs who study the paranormal using scientific methods. Founded by Lady Alouette Sarte.
- **The 3 planes**— Physical where living humans reside; the Beyond, a transitional place where ghosts reside when not in the physical plane; and the Afterlife.
- **Ghost Talking** (not to be confused with a séance)— raises the dead to see their last memories through a ritual used by those trained by the Morpheus Society.
- **Spirit Projection**— this is a moving mind-image (Ghost Talking) that can be created from the recently dead through a Ghost Talk.
- **Repeater**— a ghost attached to a specific place. Reenacts the same behavior and usually is not intelligent.
- **Gray Lady**— a female ghost usually associated with a place or family. Her appearance carries a warning message.
- **Noise Ghost**— a Poltergeist that uses energy from the living to cause trouble.
- **Possession**— A ghost inhabiting a human body and taking control of it. An uncommon occurrence and usually short term in duration due to the amount of energy a ghost needs to maintain a connection with a human.

- **Binding**— when a living person holds a soul captive because of powerful emotions. This prevents the dead one from transitioning to the Afterlife.
- **Attachment**— when a ghost won't let go of a living person or an obsession and exists in the Beyond, refusing to transition to the Afterlife.
- **Death Remembered**— sentimental jewelry for mourning, often holding a photo or lock of hair of the deceased.
- **Sundering**— a process in which the soul is destroyed so it can no longer exist in any of the three plans: earthly, Beyond, or Afterlife.

Countries:

- **Sarnesse** (Sar-nessie)— a land of rolling hills, with an extensive coastline. Vineyards. Provinces. **King Guénard** (Gie-nar) is the ruler with an elected parliament.
- **Zulskaya** (Zul-sky-a)— the closest neighbor with a large land border. Mountainous.
- **Perino** (Pa-rin-o)— a country of tropical rain forest, separated from Sarnesse by an ocean.

Addresses:

- **Madame** (Ma-dahm)— address for any financially independent and professional woman or those who are married. Any woman managing her own household. Also, A spinster would be addressed as madam.
- **Mys** (Miss)— address for financially dependent young ladies, and unmarried débutantes. Typically denotes an immaturity in the title of address.

- **Lady**— address denotes a woman of upper class, nobility.
- **Mysir** (my-sur)— address to any man, suitable for all social levels.
- **Lord**— address to any man of clear nobility, or title.

www.ingramcontent.com/pod-product-compliance
Lightning Source LLC
Chambersburg PA
CBHW061308210726
48293CB00003B/1164